The **Ghost** Adventures *of*
ORION O'BRIEN

Published by Mission Point Press
2554 Chandler Rd.
Traverse City, MI 49696
(231) 421-9513
www.MissionPointPress.com

Cover art by Mark Pate

ISBN 978-1-961302-16-7
Library of Congress Control Number 2023916515

Printed in the United States of America

The **Ghost** Adventures *of*

ORION O'BRIEN

THE PHANTOMS OF WAKARUSA

FRAN BORIN

MISSION POINT PRESS

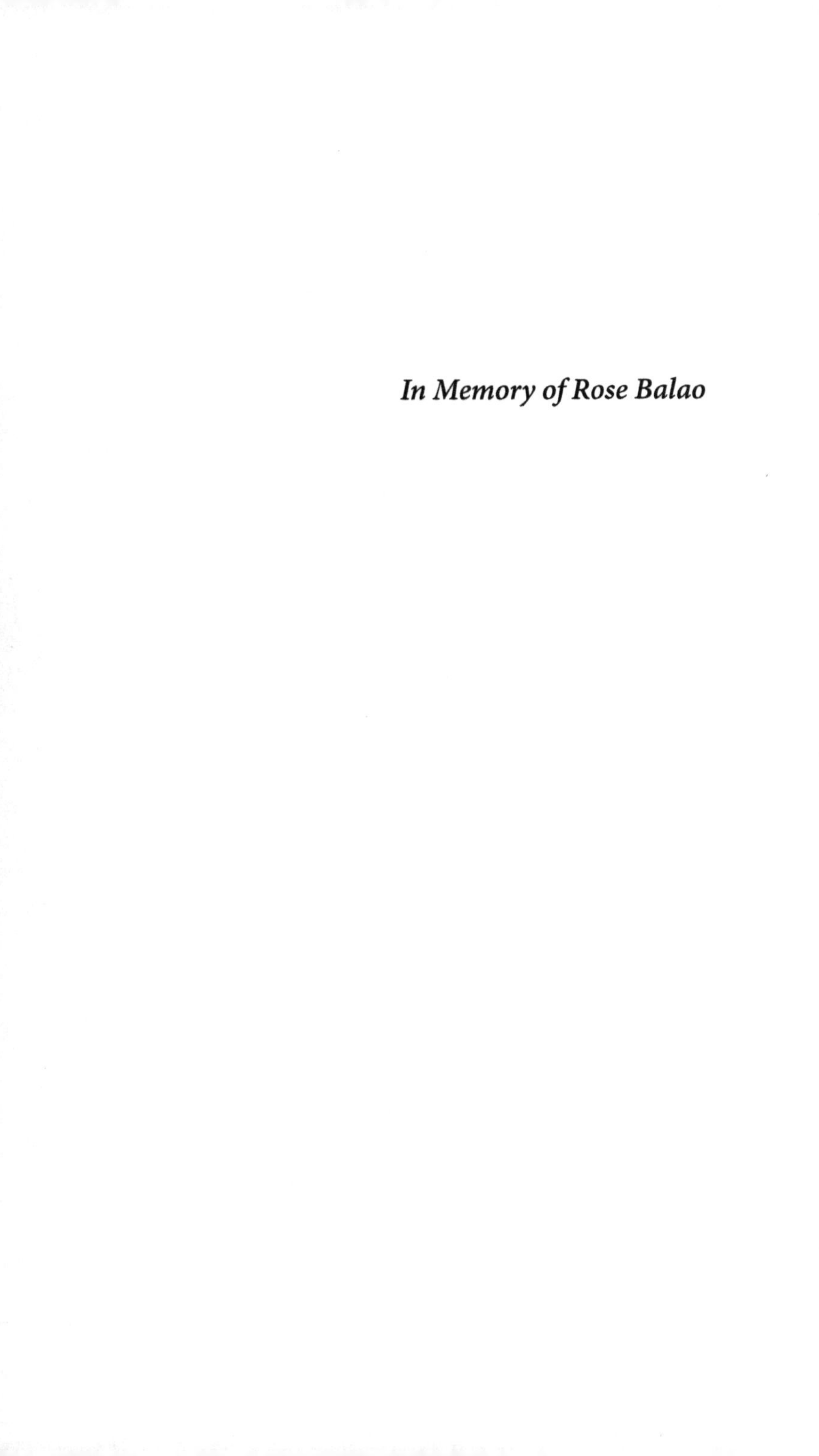

In Memory of Rose Balao

Prologue

**The Wakarusa Valley, Douglas County, Kansas:
August 1863**

"**N**oah! I got five eggs today!" Katie Wheeler announced happily to her brother. The hens flapped down from their nests and pecked greedily at the dried corn she had put down for them, while Katie gathered the eggs into her apron.

Noah didn't look up from the stool where he sat milking the cow, but muttered, "That's good, Katie."

Katie could tell Noah was upset. Any other day he would tease her, saying, "Just enough for me, too bad you won't get any!" or something like that. She guessed it was because he'd argued with Papa—again—before he came out to the barn. She wanted desperately to make

Noah happy, and said, "We'll have a good breakfast, won't we?"

Noah hardly heard his sister's voice. His mind wasn't on breakfast, or the cow or the chickens, or anything else on this godforsaken farm. All he could think about was the heated argument he'd had with his father before coming out to milk. Heated on his part, at least. Papa never raised his voice, was always reasonable, and as usual, had the last word. Noah had stalked off to the barn and closed the door, trying to shut out his father's words.

The argument was the same one they had almost every day now. Noah was itching to get off the farm and start preparing for a career as a teacher, or even a professor, like Papa. He was only thirteen, but Papa was helping him with his Greek and Latin, and he loved mathematics. If he could go back to Boston, he could stay with Uncle Wesley and prepare to go to Harvard.

But Papa wanted Noah to stay on the farm until he was fourteen and then enroll at Baker, the first four-year university in Kansas. Papa was proud to be teaching there, but as far as Noah could tell, the students were nothing special, and they even admitted young ladies! He longed to rub shoulders with the sons of lawyers and bankers and ministers at Harvard. How, he had asked, would another year of following a plow and pitching hay help him become the man he wanted to be?

"Ah, but it's the principle," said Papa. "The future of this country is moving west. We'll need educated people here, even more than back in Boston."

The principle. It always came back to that—the reason they had come to Kansas in the first place. Papa was an Abolitionist who had eagerly moved his family west to help stop the spread of slavery. After years of violence along the Missouri border, Kansas had finally entered the Union as a free state two years earlier. Noah was grateful for that. Why then, he asked, couldn't they go back to Boston now?

His thoughts were interrupted by shouts and the sound of horses galloping into the barnyard where his father was hitching up the wagon. He heard a man's voice say, "Amos Wheeler?" followed by Papa's polite reply. Probably someone from a neighboring farmstead who needed Papa's help. Noah shut the voices out.

As Katie chattered on to her hens, Noah was startled at the sound of a gunshot. Suddenly his senses were on high alert. Milk pail forgotten, he leaped to his feet, angry with himself for shutting the barn door. Then he smelled the smoke. He looked up in alarm and saw a gray cloud billowing from the hay in the loft.

Fairway, Kansas:
Present Day

Chapter 1
A Visit to the Farm

How come some people see ghosts but others don't? Is it like a super-power? Or maybe it's the ghosts who can, you know, pick and choose who can see them. But why do they choose who they do? Trust me, I've thought about this *a lot*, because a year ago, starting fifth grade, I thought people who saw ghosts were weird or crazy…or liars. But then it happened to me, and by the end of the year I'd seen not just one, but *two* ghosts—in person!

Let me bring you up to speed: my name's Orion O'Brien, and I met the ghost of Samuel Grayhawk, a Native American boy, in our neighbors' basement. He went to school in the 1840s at the Shawnee Indian Mission a few blocks from my house. He was one of the best friends I'll ever have.

Then over spring break I saw Susanna Chase (Susie for short) in a mirror in my great-grandma's attic. She escaped from slavery on the Underground Railroad and came to Quindaro, in Kansas. I'll never forget her—in fact, she turned out to be part of my family!

Just to be clear, it wasn't only me who met Samuel and Susie. My little brother Ollie, and our neighbors Sal and Sofi Martelli, were all in on it. It was the awesomest thing ever. We learned so much, not just about the way people lived back then, but about what's really important, like your family and friends, and doing the right thing. But in the end, Samuel and Susie had to go away—they're dead, after all—and life went on. Summer came and I was looking forward to sixth grade, my last year at Konza School.

But sometimes, like before I went to sleep at night, I'd wonder why, out of all the kids in the world, did Samuel and Susie come to me? I didn't tell the others, but secretly, I thought I had *the power*. Well—my dad has this thing he says: *if I knew then what I know now…*

"How would you like to spend a few days with Uncle Jeff and Aunt Abby?" Dad asked one night at dinner. "You can stay there while we paint your bedrooms. It'll be like a mini-vacation before school starts."

Ollie and I had picked out new colors for our rooms

(lavender for me, orange for him), and Mom promised me a new bedspread to match.

"*Out there?*" I asked. Uncle Jeff is my dad's older brother, and he and Aunt Abby live on a farm about an hour's drive away. "It's in the middle of nowhere!"

"It's not the middle of nowhere," said Mom. "It's just a few miles from Lawrence. They have internet and WiFi, you know. Uncle Jeff and Aunt Abby would love to have some kids around now that your cousins are all grown up. And, it'll be good for you to see what life is like on a farm."

Oh, no, if Mom says it's good for me, I know I'll hate it!

"But what is there to do?" I asked. "There's only a few days left of summer, and my friends are all here, and…"

"Well," said Mom, "you can do something to help Konza School. The PTA's big bake sale is coming up. Uncle Jeff has a blueberry patch, and you can pick blueberries to bring back for pies."

"Can't we get blueberries at the store?" I asked. My mind raced, thinking how to get out of this. Mom gave me one of those looks. "Maybe I could take Butterscotch." I'd been teaching our rescue mutt to do some tricks over the summer. That'd give me something better to do than picking blueberries.

"Not this time," said Dad. "She'll be fine without you for a few days."

"Do I have a choice?" I asked.

"Not really," he said.

So, the next Sunday we loaded our stuff in the car and drove to the farm. I'd packed my sketch pad and colored pencils, some books and our Amazon Fire to keep from dying of boredom. Ollie brought a football and a bazillion Legos. He actually seemed excited about the trip.

I knew we were there when we came to a sign by the road that said "O'Briens' Blueberries." We drove up a long gravel driveway to the house and parked at the back, in front of an old barn.

As we stepped out of the car, a big, furry black-and-brown dog came running out of the barn, barking like crazy. Uncle Jeff followed him.

"Quiet!" he said, and the dog stopped barking. "He always barks when someone new comes to the house." The dog sniffed at us, and Dad said he probably smelled Butterscotch.

"What's his name?" asked Ollie as he patted the dog.

"That's Barker," said Aunt Abby as she came out the back door of the house.

"Barker?" I asked. "Why—oooh, I get it!" Barker wagged his tail and nuzzled up to us, begging us to pet him.

Uncle Jeff took us to our cousin Bailey's old room and

showed us where to put our stuff. The minute Ollie saw there were bunk beds, he shouted, "I get the top bunk!" I didn't even argue—he always gets what he wants. Then we went to the kitchen, where Mom and Aunt Abby were lining up a bunch of jars on the counter.

"Aunt Abby's been canning carrots," said Mom. "You can take them down to the cellar for her."

I sighed out loud. *We've been here five minutes and we have to work already?*

"It won't kill you," said Mom. Somehow she always knows what I'm thinking.

"I'll show you where it is," said Aunt Abby with a smile. She's kinda plump and has red hair, and she's so friendly it's hard not to like her. She handed each of us a jar of carrots and led us to a room off the kitchen, like a back porch, but indoors. Barker's bed was there beside the washer and dryer.

Aunt Abby pulled up on a handle on one of the floorboards, and a giant black hole opened up—seriously! I mean it, all I could see were a couple of wooden steps that disappeared into darkness. Aunt Abby started down the steps.

I motioned for Ollie to follow her, but he stayed put. "Go on," I said.

"Why don't *you* go?"

"What's the problem?" asked Mom from the kitchen. Then a light clicked on down below. What could I do?

It creeped me out, but I went down the steps, and Ollie followed.

"Is this a cave?" he asked when he got to the bottom.

"It's like the dungeon of a castle!" I said. The ceiling was only about a foot above my head, and the dim light made our shadows look big and freaky. The wall behind the steps was made of rocks, but the other walls were… dirt. It smelled musty and damp and the chilly air gave me goose bumps. I looked into the dark space under the stairs and wondered what might be hiding there.

Chapter 2

The Cellar ~ *and* ~ The Hayloft

Jars of food were stacked on wooden shelves on three sides of the room. There was probably enough to last for a year.

"Actually, it is a cave," said Aunt Abby. "People dug them in the ground to keep food in, back before they had refrigerators. They also used them for shelter from tornadoes and storms. This one was outside the old log cabin that stood here. It's been here since the 1850s."

"Did you used to live in the log cabin?" asked Ollie.

"No," laughed Aunt Abby. "It's been gone for years. There was a farmhouse here after that, and finally they built this house right over the cave. We use it as a cellar."

She showed us where to put the jars and asked us to bring the rest of them down. On our next trip to the cellar, I said to Ollie, "This must be like where Samuel died." The first ghost we met, Samuel Grayhawk, crawled into a cellar after he was thrown off a horse. He died there, and years later, our neighbors' house was built over it.

"It makes me feel funny," said Ollie.

"Oooh, do you think somebody died down here?" I laughed. "I bet you're afraid a skeleton's gonna jump out at you!"

"I am not!" said Ollie, "But it's like somebody's watching me."

"Yeah, like mice or rats!" I shivered.

He walked around, touching the walls and looking under the shelves. "Something's hiding here."

"You're starting to sound wacko," I said.

"Yes!" he cried suddenly. "Here it is!" He was on his knees under the steps, wiggling one of the rocks near the dirt floor. He pulled it out and we saw a dark hole in the wall.

"Don't put your hand in there!" I said, but it was too late. He reached in the hole and pulled out an ancient-looking bowl. It was covered with dust so thick you couldn't tell what color it was. A dirty, tattered rag was inside it. He held it up to me.

"I'm not touching that!" I said. "What if there's a snake or something in there?"

Just then Aunt Abby called down the steps.

"Everything OK down there? There's a few more jars to take down."

Ollie shoved the bowl back into the hole and pushed the rock back in place. We ran up to the kitchen and took the rest of the jars to the cellar as fast as we could.

"I need sunshine," I said when we were finished. Ollie grabbed his football and we headed for the back door with Barker.

"Stay out of the hayloft," called Uncle Jeff. "And don't go into the trees."

The last time I was at the farm was Thanksgiving when I was seven or eight, and all I remembered was playing games after dinner with my cousins. Now I looked around, wondering what I would do for a week. There weren't any other houses nearby, just a gigantic yard with trees and fields all around.

If I'm gonna be stuck here, I might as well explore the place...

Barker ran toward the barn and we followed. It was humongous—at least twice as big as the house. You could tell it used to be red, but now most of the paint was worn off. The gray wooden boards had cracks and knotholes in them, and the hinges on the doors were all rusty. A huge door was standing open, so we went in.

I liked the smell inside, kind of sweet and grassy. The dirt floor was covered with straw. Uncle Jeff's SUV was parked beside a dusty black pickup truck, and tools and ropes hung on the walls. In some stalls at the back I saw a riding lawnmower and a wheelbarrow and some bales of straw, but no animals. A long worktable by the door had more tools on top and a big scale for weighing things, like at the grocery store.

"Look—chickens!" called Ollie. He was looking through a door made out of wire.

I went to see the chickens. There were white ones and brown ones standing around a room at the corner of the barn, and we could see a few more through a little door that led outside. There were shelves on the walls with boxes full of straw.

"Do they sleep in those boxes?" asked Ollie.

"It's their nests," I said.

"Aren't there any horses or cows or anything?" asked Ollie.

"I guess not," I said. As I turned to look around the rest of the barn, I noticed a sort of glow under a row of nests. I was about to go in and check it out, but stopped—*eeuw!*—when I saw chicken poop on the floor. A second later the whole room lit up when the sun came out from behind a cloud.

"A ladder!" said Ollie. He was already climbing up some boards nailed to the wall beside the chickens' door. There was a big opening in the ceiling above our heads, so I went up too.

At the top was one giant room with window holes at each end. It was like an attic, with rafters running from one end of the barn to the other. Hay bales were stacked near one of the windows.

"Must be the hayloft," I said.

"This would make a perfect Ninja Warrior gym!" cried Ollie. "Look how big it is!"

"Uncle Jeff told us to stay out," I said.

He made a pouty face. "I'll just take a little look," he said as he stepped up off the ladder.

Well, I couldn't let him go all alone, could I? By the time I stepped into the hayloft, Ollie was already at the back wall, pushing on it. Suddenly I saw daylight as the wall opened up, and Ollie was about to go over the edge!

I screamed and ran over to grab his shoulder just in time. I peeked out and saw another ladder that led to the ground, a long way down.

"I wasn't gonna fall out," he said, jerking his shoulder out of my hands.

The back wall had two doors that opened from the sides like giant shutters. Ollie held on to the top of one of the doors and stepped along the crossbeam at the bottom, out over the barnyard. "Wow!" he yelled. "This's like flying!"

I walked out along the other door, and I could see the whole farm—a big rectangle with trees on three sides, different-colored fields, and paths going around and through them. This could be the perfect place to practice my running—at least one thing I could do while I was here.

"Let's follow the path all the way around," I said. I walked my way back into the hayloft and headed for the ladder. "Shut the doors, OK?"

I was halfway down the ladder when I heard Ollie running, then a thump on the floor above me.

"Whoa!" Ollie cried out. "That almost hit me."

I poked my head back up to see what happened. Ollie was standing by the stack of hay bales, but one bale was on the floor.

"You knocked a hay bale off?" I asked.

"I didn't knock it off!" he said. "It just fell down right in front of me!"

"You jarred it loose when you were running," I said. "Come on, let's go."

Chapter 3
The Mystery Girl

We climbed back down and started out the door when Ollie stopped.

"Where's my football?" he asked. "I put it right here by the ladder." Instead of looking for it, he just stood there acting clueless.

I sighed, 'cause I knew he wouldn't let me do anything else until we found it. It wasn't on the worktable, so I started looking on the floor. There it was under the pickup truck, behind a front tire. I pulled it out and held it over my head.

"I didn't put it there!" cried Ollie as he grabbed for the football. "Somebody hid it while we were in the hayloft!"

"Like who?" I asked. It did seem weird, 'cause we'd

only been in the hayloft for five minutes and nobody else was in the barn. "Maybe Barker sniffed at it and it rolled under the truck. Let's go."

We went around behind the barn and took a good look. The garden was off to our left. The path started at the far corner, beside one of the tallest trees I'd ever seen, with leaves that glittered in the sun. I looked back at the barn to get my bearings, and saw the hayloft doors standing open.

"You were supposed to close those doors," I said.

"I did," said Ollie. He turned to look. "Remember? The hay bale fell off after I shut them."

I thought back. The doors *had* been shut when the hay bale fell off. "But we weren't supposed to be up there," I said, "so go close them." I pointed to the ladder on the side of the barn.

"Why don't *you* do it?" he asked, but then he ran to the ladder. While I waited, I looked around the far corner of the barn and saw a gigantic tub of water. Beside it was a tall, funny-looking metal thing with a long handle. I was wondering what it was when I realized Ollie hadn't come back.

I was about to yell for him to hurry up when he came around from the front of the barn.

"It's about time," I said.

"There's a girl in the hayloft," he said.

"There is not!"

"There is!" he said. "She's standing by the hay bales. Go look for yourself!"

"You better not be lying," I said as I climbed the outside ladder and pulled one of the doors open a few inches. I looked all around the hayloft, but—no surprise—didn't see anybody.

"There's no girl up there," I said when I got back down. "Come on, we're wasting time!"

I started off at a jog so he could keep up with me. We went uphill along the garden, then came to a fenced-in field full of thick, snakey vines with huge leaves. The path turned to the right along a row of sunflowers with a wall of trees behind them. We came to another fenced-in field that had rows and rows of bushes, and there were people in there with buckets.

"Must be the blueberries," I said. From there the path split in two directions, one straight ahead and one off to the right, back toward the barn.

"Are we going all the way around?" asked Ollie.

"I am," I said. "You can go back to the barn if you want." So Ollie took off down the path to the barn and I went on around the whole farm. I ran past a long field with leafy green stuff growing in it, then turned back toward the barn. I finished by a field of these tall weeds that looked like greenish squirrel tails.

I stopped there and saw Ollie looking toward a bunch of trees at the side of the yard.

"Look! Apples!" I said as I ran over to him. There were yellow, red and green ones on the trees. Ollie just stared.

"That girl's over there behind that tree," he said.

"Really?" I said. "So show me. If you're lying again, I'm telling Mom."

He ran toward the tree, but stopped short when a shiny green apple fell right in front of him. I looked up and saw a small girl with long, white-blond hair sitting in the tree. She was trying to hide in the leaves.

"That's her!" cried Ollie. "How'd she climb up there so fast?"

Just then another apple fell. I looked down for just a second—honest!—and when I looked back up, the girl was gone.

"Where'd she go?" asked Ollie. He looked up into the branches of the apple tree.

"She must've just gone up higher," I said. "Why do you care?"

"Did you see how weird she looks?"

"I hardly saw her," I said. "She looked dirty…she's probably with the berry pickers."

"But she, like, *glows*," he said.

I laughed. "She doesn't glow—you just saw the sun shining on her."

"She's in the shade, and she glowed up in the hayloft,

where it was dark!" he said. "And I could kinda see *through* her."

"You need your eyes checked," I said as we walked back toward the barn.

"She left the doors open again," said Ollie.

I sighed, beginning to wish we'd stayed out of the hayloft. I climbed up the outside ladder and started to pull one of the doors shut when something big and gray swooped down at my head and out the other door.

"YIIIIIKES!" I screamed, ducking my head. "What was that?"

Ollie stared up with his mouth hanging open, then started laughing his head off. "You should see your face!" he said. "It was just a big bird! It flew out over the garden."

"You can stop laughing any time now," I said. As I pulled the other door shut and turned to look out from the top of the ladder, I saw white-blond hair high up in the apple tree.

Mom and Dad stayed for dinner. We had burgers, corn on the cob from Aunt Abby's garden, and choco-late cake.

I'd been feeling a little nervous about staying with Uncle Jeff and Aunt Abby. I didn't actually know them very well, but they made us feel right at home. I knew they were older than Mom and Dad, but they seemed younger, maybe because they wore scruffy cutoff jeans and T-shirts. I noticed for the first time how much Uncle Jeff looks like my dad, except with gray in his hair. They talk a lot alike, too.

Uncle Jeff told us the rules about staying at the farm:

Don't drink out of the rain barrel (the big tub of water)

Don't let the chickens out of the roost (that's the room with the nests)

Wash the apples before you eat them

Don't go into the trees without permission

"What about the hayloft?" I asked.

"You can go up there," he said, "but stay back from the edge if you open the side doors. We don't want any-body falling out."

I didn't look at Ollie.

"Why don't you have any animals?" asked Ollie. "I mean, besides the chickens, like, horses or cows?"

"We're teachers, not farmers," said Aunt Abby. "We just like to live in the country, where it's peaceful and we can grow some of our own food."

"Do you eat that green stuff in the field across from the barn?" I asked.

"That's alfalfa," said Uncle Jeff. We laughed at the funny name. "No, the neighbors cut it to feed their horses.

"School starts for us soon, too," he went on.

"Farming's a full-time job, and we don't have time for it during the school year. The garden and the blueberry patch keep us busy all summer."

"And we open the pumpkin patch on weekends in the fall," said Aunt Abby.

"There's a pumpkin patch?" said Ollie. "Can I pick out a pumpkin for Halloween?"

"Sure," said Uncle Jeff. "Find the one you want, and you can come pick it when it's ready."

As we finished dinner, Dad said, "Remember to be good houseguests. That means helping with chores and cleaning up after yourselves."

"And watch your attitude," said Mom.

"I'll be a super houseguest!" cried Ollie. I almost choked on my chocolate cake.

Chapter 4

A Voice in the Night ~ *and* ~ Jeremiah

I expected Ollie to whine when Mom and Dad left, but he waved goodbye, then skipped along with Uncle Jeff as we went to take care of the chickens. First we swept the dirty straw out of the roost and scattered clean straw on the floor. We put chicken feed in some metal trays on the floor. Then Uncle Jeff took us out to the pump—that tall, rusty thing with the long handle I'd seen earlier— and showed us how to pump water. We filled jars for the chickens and a bowl for Barker.

"Is it OK to drink the pump water?" asked Ollie.

"It's fine, because the well water comes from a spring," said Uncle Jeff. "But the rain barrel has dirt and dust in it."

After that we explored the house. It was a lot different

from ours—all the rooms were on the same floor, and the bedrooms had carpets that felt good on our bare feet. Instead of a dining room, the table was in a great big kitchen that had two sinks and the biggest stove I'd ever seen. Aunt Abby said she needed the space for all the canning she did.

Bailey's room had a door that went right into the bathroom. Ollie went in to brush his teeth, and called out, "There's another room at the other end of the bathroom!"

"That's Brent's room," said Aunt Abby. "He and Bailey shared the bathroom." She turned on a night light by the mirror. "If you need anything, you know Uncle Jeff and I are right across the hall. Get a good night's sleep!"

I went in to brush my teeth and almost gagged. The sink looked like a mud pit.

"Ollie! That sink is disgusting!" I yelled. I moved my toothbrush and cup to the other sink.

Ollie was standing on the top bunk, showing off how he could touch the ceiling.

"I need bunk beds in my room!" he said. "I could have Pete and Jack sleep over!"

"Like I want *more* fourth-grade boys at my house?" I said. I turned off the light and looked out between the slats of the window shade. The barn made a black shape against the night sky.

"It sure is dark out here, with no streetlights like at home."

Ollie leaned over from the top bunk to look out.

"Hey, there's a light on in the barn," he said.

He was right—light was coming through the cracks between the boards in the chickens' roost.

"The chickens must have a night light," I said.

"Do you think that girl we saw hid my football?" he asked as he settled in on the top bunk.

"Maybe," I said. "Anyway, she's gone now. Go to sleep."

I WAS DREAMING. I was at a soccer game and my friend Taylor was bugging me to go talk to the referee, her brother's friend.

"NO!" *Wait, did I say that?*

"NO!" *There it was again…Ollie?*

My eyes snapped open. Ollie was thrashing around in the top bunk. I couldn't remember him ever having nightmares, but I knew I'd better check on him—I'm the big sister, right? I stood on the edge of the bottom bunk and grabbed his arm. "Ollie!" I whispered. "Stop yelling, you'll wake up Uncle Jeff!"

He opened his eyes and blinked in the dim light.

"Are you having a nightmare?" I asked.

"Orion?" he said. "Somebody's talking to me! Didn't you hear it?"

"All I heard was you, yelling 'No!' What did you dream?"

"They kept saying, 'Go away! Go away!' and 'Don't touch it!'"

"Don't touch what?" I asked. "Who said it?"

"I don't know," he said. "A bigger boy, maybe? I couldn't see his face."

"It was just a dream," I said. "You're fine. Go back to sleep."

He flopped back down in bed, and I didn't hear anything the rest of the night.

MONDAY MORNING WE SMELLED SOMETHING AWESOME AS SOON AS WE WOKE UP. We went straight to the kitchen, and Uncle Jeff said, "Come on, if you want breakfast, you have to gather the eggs!"

"Is that homemade bread I smell?" I asked. I know, because our neighbor Betty back home makes it all the time.

In the barn we put out fresh feed for the chickens. When they fluttered down to the floor to eat, we saw eggs in their nests! The white chickens laid white eggs and the brown ones laid brown eggs! We had scrambled eggs and homemade bread with strawberry jam for breakfast.

"Are we picking blueberries today?" asked Ollie as he stuffed bread in his mouth.

"Not today," said Aunt Abby. "Lots of people are coming today and tomorrow, so we'll have you wait a couple of days."

After breakfast I went out to run the path again. After that, Aunt Abby called us to come help in the garden. She handed Ollie some baskets and sent me to the barn to get the wheelbarrow.

Uncle Jeff was waiting by the barn door for the people coming to pick blueberries. He had someone with him.

"Orion, this is Jeremiah. He helps me keep track of the blueberry picking, and other things around the farm, so if you see him in the barn or the fields, you'll know it's OK," said Uncle Jeff. "If you need help with anything, you can always ask him."

Jeremiah was as tall as Uncle Jeff but I could tell he was a teenager. He wore ratty shorts, a T-shirt with the sleeves ripped out and a backwards Kansas City Royals baseball cap. "Hi," I said. He nodded at me but then looked down and didn't say anything.

I got the wheelbarrow and took it to the garden, which was bigger than our front and back yards put together. A zillion things were growing there—corn, green beans, tomatoes, peppers, cucumbers, zucchini, carrots, lettuce, and even more. We picked green beans, tomatoes and corn. Aunt Abby showed us how to tear the husks off the ears of corn and pull the silk out to get it ready for canning. We filled the wheelbarrow and Ollie wheeled it back to the kitchen door.

By then Uncle Jeff was almost finished mowing the grass with the riding lawnmower, and he let me drive it to the barn door. Then he showed Ollie how to cut corn stalks with a big knife that looked like a machete. Ollie pretended he was hacking his way through the jungle.

Aunt Abby called to tell us lunch was almost ready. "Why don't you go look at the pumpkins now, before lunch?" she said. "They're in the fenced-in field just north of the garden." She pointed. "You can't miss them."

The pumpkin patch was the one with the snakey vines and curly leaves. Ollie climbed over the wooden gate in the fence.

"You could just unlatch it, you know," I said as I opened the gate.

He was already digging through the vines. All of a sudden he yelled, "Look at this!" Underneath some leaves there was a shiny green thing the size of a soccer ball. "Is that a pumpkin?" he asked. "It's so…green!"

There were green balls everywhere, in all sizes, some as big as a basketball. They had dark green stripes down the sides.

"Hey," I said, "there's one starting to turn orange!"

"Yes!" said Ollie. "I'm picking mine out now!"

"Yeah, me too!" I said.

The vines had little whiskery hairs on them that scratched our fingers, but we looked through them until we found the pumpkins we wanted—a long, skinny one for Ollie and a fat, round one for me.

Ollie frowned. "How will we remember which ones they are?"

"Uh…good question." I looked at the line of trees behind the sunflowers. "Go find some sticks and we'll stick them in the ground beside the pumpkins. I'll stay here and keep track of them."

Ollie went out the gate, ducked through the sunflowers, and came back after a few minutes with two sticks. As we stuck them in the ground, we heard somebody laughing. It sounded like it came from behind the sunflowers.

Chapter 5

Eyes in the Trees ~ *and* ~ The Ninja Warrior Hayloft

"**W**as there somebody back in the trees?" I asked.

"How should I know?" he said. "I didn't go in—remember the rule?"

"I *know*," I said, "but what if somebody else is there? Let's look." We retraced Ollie's path back to the edge of the trees. I could see why we weren't supposed to go in. It was like a forest, with trees and bushes and vines so thick you could hardly squeeze through. I took a few *tiny* steps in (well, maybe more than a few). It was like a whole 'nother world—dark and quiet and totally cut off from outside.

I took another step and felt my foot slip forward. Before I knew it I was on my butt, skidding toward the edge of a steep drop-off. I got hold of a little tree trunk just in time. As I stood up, Ollie came pushing past me and I grabbed his shirt before he went over the edge.

"Listen, I hear water," I said. "There must be a creek down there."

Ollie turned back to me. "Somebody's watching me," he said.

"Who—" Before I could finish something crashed into the bushes behind us.

I whipped around so fast my feet slipped near the edge again, but I managed to stop myself. Barker came panting up behind us.

"Barker, you scared me half to death!" I cried. My heart was pounding and I wondered why Ollie wasn't cracking up, but he was staring down into the trees.

"Look right there!" He grabbed my arm and pointed. "See their eyes?" he said. "That's who we heard laughing!"

I looked where he was pointing, but all I saw were leaves and vines in the dark shade.

"I don't see anybody," I said. Barker was wagging his tail and sniffing the ground. I scratched his head. "And Barker's not barking, so there can't be anybody there."

We clawed our way out of the trees and as I blinked in the sunshine, I saw long blond hair almost hidden in the sunflowers.

"Look!" I said. "There's that girl again! That must be who we heard laughing."

"It didn't sound like a little kid," said Ollie. "And why is she still here, anyway? It's like she's following me!"

It did seem weird that her parents let her wander off by herself. "I think she's just trying to hide from us," I said. "Come on, I'm hungry."

We raced back to the house, and I let Ollie win, which wasn't easy since he's a foot shorter than me.

"Let's get a drink of water from the pump," said Ollie.

We took turns pushing the pump handle down. I was catching water in my hands for a deep drink when suddenly Ollie stopped pumping.

"Hey!" I yelled. "I'm not finished!"

I looked up and saw the little blond girl staring at us from behind the rain barrel. It was the first time I'd gotten a good look at her. She was wearing an ugly long brown dress with an apron over it, and she was dirty all over. As soon as I saw her, she turned and disappeared around the corner of the barn.

"Did you see how she glows?" asked Ollie.

I *had* noticed a kind of whitish light all around her, and something else—it was almost like I could see through her, but that just didn't make sense. "It's the bright sun," I said. "It makes our eyes play tricks on us."

"Well, *you* don't glow in the bright sun," said Ollie.

"And besides, you know how you can see things in the water, like a mirror? I could see the side of the barn in the rain barrel, but *not her*!"

"You're losing your mind," I said. I couldn't help wondering, though, how she got to the pump before we did.

After lunch we took bottles of ice water and went to the hayloft. I took my drawing things, to start making a map of the farm, and Ollie took a shoebox full of Legos. We pushed the big doors open and I dangled my legs out with my sketch pad on my lap. Ollie sat beside me, building something out of Legos. He said it was a space station. It looked like a box with arms.

"So how do you like the farm so far?" I asked. "It's not as bad as I thought it would be."

"It's fun," he said, then looked up from his Legos. "But I still think somebody's watching me."

"If you mean that little girl, she's probably just curious," I said.

"It's not her!" he said. "I felt it in the cellar yesterday, too! Haven't you ever felt like that?" he asked.

"Yeah, in second grade when I copied off Emma Drake's spelling test," I said. "Mrs. Crenshaw had her eye on me for *weeks*!"

Ollie shrugged, then pointed at the rafters across the top of the hayloft.

"This'll be a great Ninja Warrior gym," he said. "If I could get up there, I could swing clear across the barn!" He climbed up on the hay bales, but he still couldn't reach the rafters.

"Go down and get one of those ropes off the wall," I said. "We can throw it over the rafter so you can climb up it."

Ollie scrambled down the ladder and came back after a few minutes with a long rope.

"What's the dude's name you told me about? He's down there putting blueberries on the scale," he said.

"Jeremiah," I said.

"He's like a body-builder! His muscles are really ripped!" said Ollie.

"Whatever," I said. I was measuring in my mind how far it was to the rafters. I'd seen how Dad put a rope in our tree house, so I made a slip knot in one end of the rope. I stood on the hay bales and threw it over the closest rafter, then pulled the other end through the loop. Ollie climbed it with no trouble.

"You're on your own now."

I went back to the door to work on my map, which was turning out pretty good. I saw Ollie swinging hand-over-hand on the rafters out of the corner of my eye.

"Y-I-I-I-E-E-E!"

Chapter 6

Ollie's Bad Day ~ *and* ~ The Ouija Board

I jumped at the ear-splitting yell. When I looked up I saw the rope swinging back and forth with Ollie halfway down.

"Cut the superhero act!" I shouted. "You could've made me fall out!"

"Help me!" he yelled. "It won't stop!"

That's when I knew he wasn't playing. The rope looked like somebody was yanking on it, while Ollie hung on for dear life. I ran over and grabbed the rope. It pulled me with it as it swung back, but I got it to stop.

"Couldn't you just slide straight down?" I asked.

"I tried to!" he said as he dropped off the rope. "It, like, came alive!"

"Ropes *do not* come alive," I said. "Do you think you're in the jungle or something?"

Ollie looked up at the rope. "I know it sounds crazy," he said, "but something weird's going on."

"You got that right—it sounds crazy."

Uncle Jeff was calling to us from down below, so we left our things in the hayloft and climbed down. He handed us some wooden stakes with our names on them and got a hammer out of the toolbox. "Pound these in beside your pumpkins so we can keep track of them," he told us. We took off for the pumpkin patch.

"Uh-oh," I said as soon as we got there. "What happened to our sticks?"

The sticks we'd put beside our pumpkins were gone. As I looked around I saw a heap of broken sticks on the ground between some vines.

"Who would do that?" Ollie asked.

I was beginning to wonder about the little blond girl, but there we were with the hammer and stakes, so I said, "Let's just find new ones."

We each picked out another pumpkin and hammered the stakes in the ground beside them. When we got back to the barn I remembered my sketch pad was still in the hayloft.

"Come on, we have to get our stuff," I said. Ollie ran ahead of me and hurried up the ladder. I'd barely started to climb when I heard him shouting. *OMG, what now?*

"Look at my space station!" he cried. "It's wrecked!" When I caught up to him, Ollie was on his knees with Legos scattered all around him.

"Whoa, it's like somebody bombed it!" I said.

"Who's doing this?" Ollie asked. "First my pumpkin, and now my Legos! Why are all these bad things happening to me?"

He was starting to sound whiny. "That's too bad," I said. "Let's go back to the house. You can build your space station again in Bailey's room."

We picked up the Legos and carted everything to the ladder. As we started climbing down, I heard someone laughing.

"There it is again!" said Ollie. "And it's not a little kid!"

He was right, it sounded like somebody…older. We looked behind the hay bales, but nobody was there. Down below, Jeremiah was at the table weighing blueberries for some people. A couple of kids about my age were with them.

"I bet those kids wrecked your space station," I said as we walked back to the house. "They could've gone up while we were in the pumpkin patch, and we never would've seen them. They probably broke our pumpkin sticks, too."

Ollie just shrugged, but I actually felt better after

seeing the kids. It made me mad that they were picking on us, but at least the mystery was solved.

"It had to be them," I said. "That's who we heard laughing, too. They're leaving now, so we'll be OK."

AUNT ABBY WAS IN THE KITCHEN CANNING CORN, so we went to Bailey's room. I started coloring in my map of the farm while Ollie nosed around in the closet.

"What's this?" he asked. He was holding an ancient-looking box with the word "OUIJA" on the top. "Ow-ja? Is it a game?"

He opened the box and unfolded a board with the alphabet on it, some numbers, and the words "YES," "NO," and "GOODBYE." I knew what it was 'cause I'd seen one at my friend Taylor's house.

"It's 'wee-jee,'" I said. "It's supposed to tell you the answers to questions, like about the future and stuff. It doesn't work, though. Taylor's sister has one, and I asked if I'd get a phone for Christmas and it said 'yes,' but I didn't."

"Let's try it!" he said.

I took the flat, triangle-shaped pointer out of the box and put it in the middle of the board.

"OK, ask it a question and put your fingers here on the pointer, like this," I said. "Then the pointer will go to the answer."

Ollie scooted up to the board and put his fingers on

the pointer with mine. "Will I be a real Ninja Warrior someday?" he asked.

I almost laughed—he was actually holding his breath! At first nothing happened, but then the pointer moved toward the top of the board to the word "YES."

"YESSS!" cried Ollie. "I'm gonna be a Ninja Warrior! OK, will the Royals win the World Series?"

Again, the pointer moved toward the word "YES."

"This is great!" he said. "Umm, I know—is Orion gonna marry Micah?"

"Shut up!" I said. "You know this isn't for real!" I grabbed for the pointer, but he whipped it away from me. As I lunged for him, I heard Aunt Abby's voice at the door.

"I'll get you for this," I whispered as she came into the room.

"Orion? Can you help me for a few minutes?" She looked at the Ouija board. "Goodness, I'd forgotten we had that," she said. "It's really old, you know—it belonged to my mother."

We went to the kitchen where I climbed on a footstool to reach a bowl on a high shelf for Aunt Abby. As I got down, Uncle Jeff and Jeremiah came in, and Ollie told them about his wrecked Legos.

"We saw some kids in the barn getting their blueberries weighed. I think they did it," I said.

"Hmmm, I doubt it," said Uncle Jeff. "Jeremiah

wouldn't let any kids go up to the hayloft. If they did, he'd tell me."

Instead of nodding, Jeremiah just looked at the floor and said nothing. I suddenly wondered…*does he already know about it?*

"But who could have done it?" asked Ollie.

Uncle Jeff thought a minute. "Maybe a raccoon? They're attracted by bright colors, and they can climb, although they usually come out at night," he said.

"But I heard someone laughing," said Ollie, "not just there but up in the pumpkin patch. And this girl's been following me around."

"Really?" said Aunt Abby. "We'll have to remind the berry pickers to keep their kids inside the fence with them. We don't want them going down to the river."

"The river?" I asked. "You mean that creek down in the trees?"

"It's the Wakarusa River," Uncle Jeff explained. "You didn't go down there, did you?"

"No, we just heard the water," said Ollie. "Can we play there?"

"I don't see why not," said Uncle Jeff. "The water's low right now because the summer's been dry, but there used to be bad floods before they built the dam upstream. We'll show you how to get down there tomorrow."

Chapter 7

Something's in the Bowl ~ *and* ~The Light in the Barn Explained

---

At dinner Uncle Jeff told us funny stories about Dad when he was growing up.

"One time he blew a big bubble gum bubble that popped in his face and stuck in his hair. Instead of telling our mom, he just cut it out, hair and all. He had a big round space with no hair right in front!"

"He never told us that!" I giggled.

"I want to show Dad how I can swing across the top of the hayloft," said Ollie. "I put up a rope so I could reach the rafters."

"*You* put up a rope?" I asked.

"That doesn't sound very safe," said Aunt Abby. "Let Uncle Jeff stack the hay bales up higher."

"Good idea," said Uncle Jeff, smiling at Ollie. "You know, you look just like your dad when he was your age." Ollie's eyes were shining—it made up for his bad day.

After we cleared the table, Aunt Abby asked us to take the jars of canned corn to the cellar. I took a jar in each hand and headed for the cellar steps, but Ollie didn't move.

"What's the matter?" I asked. "Afraid of the dark?"

"Shut up!" he yelled back. He grabbed some jars of corn and went down the steps in front of me. When we got back to the kitchen, Aunt Abby put her arm around Ollie's shoulders.

"Does the cellar scare you?" she asked. "I know it's damp and dark, but there's nothing there that can hurt you."

"I'm not scared," he said as he leaned down to cuddle Barker, then he took another jar of corn. "Orion's just making fun of me."

"Sorry," I said. I hoped Aunt Abby didn't see me roll my eyes.

We made three more trips to the cellar to put away the corn. When we were finished, Ollie got down under the steps and pulled the bowl out from the hole in the wall. Something rattled when he shook it. A cloud of dust came off the old rag as he lifted the edge, and we both stared.

"What is it?" asked Ollie.

It was like a little black hockey puck but round on the edges. A long chain was attached to it and there was a screw-like thing on one side.

"I'm not sure," I said as I picked it up. It felt heavy, like metal. When I held it up to the light bulb, I could see a few patches of silver shining through the black. There was a swirly design carved into the outside.

"It's sort of like a…a locket, you know, that you wear around your neck? But it's too big and heavy!" I noticed a groove running around the outside edge, so I stuck my thumbnail in, and it snapped open. Yes! I knew exactly what it was then. Even though it had dark splotches all over it, we could see Xs, Is and Vs spaced around the edge. Two fancy little arrows were attached in the middle.

"It's a watch!" I said. "The old-fashioned kind, see? Those letters are Roman numerals." I held it up but didn't hear any ticking. "It's gotta be ancient."

"Let me hold it," said Ollie. As soon as he touched it he gasped.

"Whoa!" he said. "It shocked me!" He dropped the watch back into my hand.

"What? How could it shock you?" I asked. He

touched the watch with one finger, then took it back in his hand.

"Not really shocked," he said. "It kinda tingled at first, but it stopped."

"Orion? Ollie? Are you finished down there?" Aunt Abby's voice came from up above. Ollie put the watch back in the bowl, covered it up with the rag, and pushed the bowl back into the wall.

"Coming!" I shouted. Before we started up the steps, he grabbed my arm.

"Don't tell them about it," he said.

"Why not?" I asked.

"Just don't."

WE HAD FUN THAT NIGHT. Uncle Jeff and Ollie had a contest to see who could build the tallest building out of marshmallows and pretzel sticks (I think Uncle Jeff let Ollie win). I looked some things up on my Amazon Fire.

"It says here that raccoons like shiny things," I said. "But some birds do, too. Maybe a bird smashed your space station."

Aunt Abby said, "I suppose it could have been the barn owl that nests up there."

"A barn owl?" I asked. *That must be what almost knocked me off the ladder.*

Ollie just sighed. "Maybe," he said.

"Come on," said Uncle Jeff. "Let's make s'mores out of the marshmallows."

That cheered Ollie up. We went to the kitchen and stacked marshmallows onto graham crackers. While they heated in the oven, we broke chocolate bars into pieces. A few minutes later we were stuffing down the s'mores.

"Do you think you two can sweep out the roost and feed the chickens by yourselves?" asked Uncle Jeff. "Don't forget to latch the door."

We jumped up to go to the barn. I was proud that Uncle Jeff trusted us with a real farm job, and wanted to do it just right.

The sun was almost down and the chickens were already sleeping in their nests when we got to the barn. We filled a scoop with feed and got ready to sweep out the old straw. That's when I saw the glow in the darkened roost. It couldn't be a ray of sunlight at this time of night!

I put my finger to my lips and pointed at the glow. We opened the door quietly and peeked under the nests. I almost screamed at what I saw.

Two bright blue eyes were looking back at us.

Chapter 8

The Mystery Girl is Caught! ~ *and* ~

The Voice Returns

"It's her!" cried Ollie.

The little blond girl was sitting cross-legged under the chickens' nests, looking scared and surprised. Close up I could see black smudges all over her clothes and in her hair. Her clothes were awful—a long brown dress and an apron with pukey yellow stains all over it. I figured she couldn't be more than seven or eight. But the weirdest thing was…I could see through her! The white glow around her made her look like she was made out of fog, or maybe smoke.

"Who are you?" asked Ollie. "Are you following me?"

The little girl didn't move as she looked from me to

Ollie. Then before I could stop her, she slipped out from under the nests and out the door of the roost. She ran a few steps, then just disappeared into thin air.

We stood there with our mouths hanging open. Finally, Ollie said, "She's a *ghost!*"

I hardly heard him, my mind was whirling so fast. A ghost *here*? And who was she? When I came to my senses I said, "Come on, we better finish up and go back in the house before Uncle Jeff starts to wonder where we are."

"Are you gonna tell him?" asked Ollie.

"Are you *serious*?" I said as we scattered the fresh straw on the floor.

We did our best to act normal. Ollie told Uncle Jeff the chickens were asleep and they had plenty of food and water. We ate a few more s'mores and went to Bailey's room.

Ollie was bouncing off the walls. "There's a ghost! There's a ghost! I *told* you there was something weird here!"

"You said someone was watching you! You never said anything about a *ghost*!" I said.

"But lots of weird stuff has happened," he said. "Like my football getting hidden, and the hay bale falling down."

"You think *she* did that stuff?"

"Well…no, but she always shows up right after something happens," he said.

"I wonder where she came from and what she's doing here."

"She's following me," he said.

"Why would she follow *you*?" I asked. "Think! Think like a ghost! What do ghosts want?"

"Samuel and Susie needed our help," he said, "but this girl ran away. She acted afraid of us."

"You're right about how she always shows up after something bad happens," I said. "So maybe she *is* watching us, you know? And now we know she hangs out in the roost. We'll try and sneak up on her tomorrow night, and get her to talk to us."

I woke out of a sound sleep to hear Ollie whacking his pillow. I looked up over the edge of his bunk.

"Wake up!" I said as I shook his shoulder. "You're dreaming again!" He kind of jumped and then opened his eyes.

"He was back," he said. "He's telling me to not touch something, but I don't know what!"

"Keep your voice down!" I whispered. I climbed up to sit on the top bunk. "Did you see who it was?"

"I think he's like a teenage boy," he said. "The voice was kinda grown up but not really."

A light bulb went on in my head. "You know what?"

I said. "I bet I know who you're dreaming about, and who wrecked your space station."

"Yeah? Who?" he asked.

"Jeremiah."

"No!" said Ollie out loud. "I know what Jeremiah looks like, and it's not him."

"SSHHHH!" I whispered. "Look, Jeremiah's a teenager and he acts real weird. Who else could it be?"

"Well…promise you won't laugh?" He was wide awake now.

"I promise," I said.

"It's a ghost."

I couldn't help it—I laughed out loud, even though I'd promised I wouldn't! "That little girl? No! Possible! Way!"

"Not her—I told you, it's a boy!" he whispered. "He was telling me to go away!"

"You think there's *another* ghost?"

"Why not?" he said. "What if he hid my football and wrecked my space station—and broke the pumpkin sticks and yanked the rope? A ghost could do all that!"

"But why?" I asked.

"I guess he doesn't like me," said Ollie.

"Listen, Uncle Jeff says Jeremiah knows everything that goes on here—that means he always knows where we are and what we're doing. He could've done all those things when we weren't there."

"How could he yank the rope?" asked Ollie. "And what about that hay bale that fell down in front of me?"

"Those were just…weird accidents! But when you were telling Uncle Jeff about your space station, Jeremiah looked at the floor, like he *already knew.* Besides, no ghost would care about Legos or pumpkins."

"But he told me not to touch something," said Ollie. "What if he means that old watch? Jeremiah doesn't know about that, does he?"

"Ummm…." I didn't have an answer for that.

"I don't care if you believe me or not," he said. "I've got a gut feeling."

"A *gut* feeling? Don't be dumb," I said. "It's all those s'mores you ate!"

"I *know* there's a ghost doing things to me! It's why I felt somebody watching me in the barn, and in the trees, and in the cellar."

"Well, *I* never felt anything weird," I said. "If there's another ghost here, wouldn't I know it?"

"No, because it hasn't done anything bad to you!" he said.

"Look, let's talk about it tomorrow. Go to sleep now."

I got back into bed, but I didn't go to sleep. I couldn't stop thinking about what Ollie had said. Could there really be another ghost?

But that wasn't what really kept me awake. OK, we had a ghost—been there and done that. No, the big problem was, I'd been taken by surprise. Why would a ghost come to Ollie and not me? Was I losing the power?

Use logic, Orion, like solving a math problem. Ollie said the voice was a teenage boy. Jeremiah's a teenager. He's always nearby when the bad things happen. He won't talk to us. It has to be him! Ollie's only nine, he'll believe what he wants to believe. I'm eleven-and-a-half now, and I know it just doesn't work that way.

One thing I knew for sure, the farm wasn't boring!

Chapter 9
A Clue in the Scale ~ *and* ~ The Wakarusa River

I had to wake Ollie up Tuesday morning. He climbed down and sat on the bottom bunk.

"Did the voice come back again?" I asked.

"No—not the boy," he said. "But that girl talked to me."

"Are you sure it was her? What did she say?" I asked.

"I'm sure it was her! She said not to be afraid," he said. "That's all I remember."

"Well, she goes everywhere. She probably saw Jeremiah smashing your Legos and breaking the pumpkin sticks, and she's telling you—" I started.

"Breakfast is ready!" Aunt Abby was at the door.

We followed her to the kitchen where she had oatmeal on the table for us.

"Did you have trouble sleeping?" she asked. "I thought I heard you in the night."

I had to think fast. "Uh, Ollie had to go to the bathroom, and I had to help him so he wouldn't fall out of the top bunk," I said. "I'm sorry if we woke you up." Ollie kicked me under the table.

Uncle Jeff came in then and said, "Did you forget to latch the roost door when you watered the chickens last night? Some of them were out in the barn this morning."

Uh-oh! Ollie and I looked at each other. "Didn't you latch it" I asked.

"I did!" he said, then, "Did any chickens get lost?"

"No, they always come back to eat," said Uncle Jeff, "but we don't want them out at night because a coyote could get them."

"We'll be more careful, I promise!" I said.

As soon as we got to the barn to gather the eggs after breakfast, I turned on Ollie. "Why didn't you latch the door? Now Uncle Jeff thinks we didn't do a good job!"

"I did!" he yelled back. "After the girl ran out, I made sure it was latched. You're just trying to get me in trouble!"

"I'll be in trouble too if the chickens get out!" I said. "Just be more careful from now on! Don't we have enough to worry about with the ghost?"

"You mean *ghosts*," said Ollie.

"Look," I said, "we've only seen one ghost. It's

Jeremiah who wrecked your Legos and broke the pumpkin sticks. There's no invisible bully out there making you have accidents."

Ollie didn't argue because Uncle Jeff came into the barn with Jeremiah. We took the eggs back to the house, then I went to run the path. As soon as I got back, Aunt Abby took us to the garden.

We dug potatoes (I never knew they grew underground!) and picked cucumbers, peppers and more tomatoes. After we loaded the wheelbarrow, we went to the apple trees and Aunt Abby had us climb up to get apples for a pie (guess which ones? The green ones!).

When Ollie and I took the wheelbarrow and tools back to the barn, I saw Jeremiah put something in the bowl of the scale, then walk off toward the garden. As soon as he was gone, I looked in the scale—and there was a blue Lego block!

I snatched it and showed it to Ollie.

"Now do you see why I think he's the one picking on you?" I asked.

Ollie stuffed the Lego into his shorts pocket but didn't say anything.

FOR LUNCH WE HAD HOT DOGS, POTATO SALAD and some carrots from the garden. Ollie even ate a few cucumbers, which he hates! Uncle Jeff asked if we were having fun.

"Uh-huh," said Ollie.

"The path is great for running, and I'm making a map of the farm," I said.

"Abby says you found the Ouija board," he said.

"It said the Royals are gonna win the World Series!" said Ollie.

Uncle Jeff laughed. "Did it say what year?"

That afternoon Aunt Abby showed us how to get to the river. A path zig-zagged down the steep bank behind the sunflowers from the edge of the blueberry patch. You could hardly see it in the thick trees and vines.

The Wakarusa didn't look anything like the big Kansas River we'd seen so many times. For one thing, you could throw a rock across it. The water fell over some rocks into a pool that was so clear you could see the bottom. A big flat rock shelf stuck out from the far bank and a dead tree had fallen on to it. It made a bridge all the way across the river. On past the dead tree, the water turned muddy and brown. Big trees on both sides made it cool and shady.

"It's a good place to play right now," said Aunt Abby, "but after heavy rains, the water sometimes comes all the way up to the blueberry patch."

Ollie went out to the middle of the pool where the water came up to his shoulders. He started to climb onto the dead tree, but Aunt Abby told him to stay off because it might be rotten. We splashed in the pool with Barker, and threw green walnuts and acorns into the water to watch them get carried away.

Aunt Abby's phone rang. "I'm going up the path where the signal's better to take this call," she said. "I'll be right back. Watch out for Ollie."

"You don't have to watch out for me!" said Ollie as he splashed water in my face.

"Don't worry, I'll keep an eye on him," I said. I dunked him under, then hopped out onto the rock shelf to see if I could find any fossil seashells. Ollie started to climb onto the dead tree again.

"Aunt Abby said to stay off."

But Ollie was already up on the tree, which didn't have any bark on it. He stood up and cannonballed into the pool.

I felt a tiny tug of guilt. Aunt Abby had asked me to watch Ollie, and he'd disobeyed. I glanced up the slope to where she'd gone, but couldn't see her.

"Don't do it again," I said. "I don't need you to drown yourself."

Ollie didn't answer, he just stood in the pool and stared at the dead tree. When he motioned to me, I jumped in beside him.

"Look!" he whispered. "Don't you see it? There's a face looking out from behind the tree—I think it's the boy from my dream! I remember now, he had dirt in his hair and all over his face. It's gotta be the other ghost!"

"I don't see anything!" I said. "And you don't know for sure there's another ghost!"

"*I* know it even if you don't!" he said. "He wrecked my space station and broke my pumpkin stick and—"

"SHHHH!" I said, looking up the path and keeping my voice low. "And *I* know it's Jeremiah! He's always slinking around the barn, he never says anything, and—"

"But somebody knocked off a hay bale, and yanked the rope, and broke the pumpkin sticks! Why don't you believe me?"

Oh, for crying out loud, I thought. "Look, I'm sorry about the things that happened to you, but we have to use our heads! If you can prove there's another ghost, I'll believe you."

"OK, I will!" he said. He swam back over to the dead tree without looking at me. "Just watch me!"

How do you reason with a nine-year-old? I was paddling back toward the rock shelf when I heard a splash. It seemed to come from down the river. When I turned to see what it was, Ollie was gone.

Chapter 10

The Invisible Bully Strikes Again ~ *and* ~

Company Comes

Oh, no! Had somebody been hiding behind the tree and grabbed him? In a panic, I scrambled over the dead tree and landed in the muddy river downstream. It wasn't deep, but the bottom was squishy and slippery. Ollie stood there, shaking his head and snorting water. I sloshed over, grabbed his arm and dragged him to the bank. His swimsuit and legs were covered with mud.

"You were supposed to stay off of the tree!" I said. "It's slippery!"

"But I didn't slip!" he said. "Something pushed me into the river!"

"You mean like an invisible hand? Don't be stupid!" I shouted, but realized yelling at him wasn't going to do any good. "You better get cleaned up before Aunt Abby sees you."

We sat on the rock shelf with our feet in the pool and washed the mud off. "It's the ghost," said Ollie.

Before I could argue I heard Aunt Abby calling to us from up the path.

"Come on," I said. I jumped off the rock to cross the pool and follow Aunt Abby, when something white on the dead tree caught my eye. I froze in my tracks—there was the ghost girl sitting on the bare trunk!

Ollie was standing in the pool like a statue. "Look at the water in front of the tree," he whispered.

Aunt Abby called again. "Coming!" I yelled. I pulled Ollie through the pool as fast as I could. The last thing I needed was for Aunt Abby to come down the path and see a ghost! Luckily, when I turned back around, she was gone. But Ollie was digging his fingers into my arm.

"Did you see?" he said under his breath. "She wasn't in the water!"

"What are you talking about?"

"Like at the rain barrel! She doesn't have any... reflection!" he said.

Aunt Abby came partway down the path. "Hey, kids, come on back to the house," she said. "Uncle Jeff called and said there's somebody here to see you."

"Who?" asked Ollie.

"A surprise," she said.

My brain worked overtime as we followed Aunt Abby to the house. Why did everything have to happen at once? Ollie fell in the river and the ghost girl showed up. Maybe she *was* doing all the bad things! I wanted to be somewhere alone so I could think, but as soon as we came over the rise in the alfalfa field, I saw Dad's car in the driveway.

"Mom and Dad are here?" I asked. *Do we have to go home already, just when we've found a ghost?*

Suddenly Ollie started running toward the house. "It's Sal!" he yelled. He was right—our neighbors Sal and Sofi were there in the driveway with my dad and Uncle Jeff. Sofi had her arms around Barker, who was wagging his tail like mad, but Sal stood off by himself, looking at the ground.

Sal and Sofi moved across the street from us last summer, and they've been in on all our ghost adventures—in fact, their basement was where we found Samuel Grayhawk. Sal's ready for sixth grade, just like me, but we've kinda gone in different directions since we met Susie (our second ghost) over spring break. I wasn't sure how I felt about him being there. I mean, I like him OK and all, but my mom goes overboard about what a great kid he is.

Dad ruffled Ollie's hair. "Hi, bud," he said. "I brought you some company. We told their mom you were here at the farm, and she asked if they could come for a few days, too. They'll help pick the blueberries for the bake sale."

"We'll change the sleeping arrangements," said Aunt Abby. "Orion, you and Sofi can stay in Bailey's room, and Ollie and Sal can sleep in Brent's room."

"But there's no bunk beds in there!" said Ollie. I smiled to myself. *I get the top bunk now!*

"No, but there's a door out to the porch. You can go outside right from the bedroom," said Aunt Abby. "Brent used to sleep out there sometimes in the summer."

Ollie's face lit up. "Let's go see!"

"Go get dry clothes on," said Aunt Abby. "I'll bet you're hungry."

I KNEW OLLIE WAS DYING TO TELL SAL ABOUT THE GHOST GIRL, but Sal shuffled along behind us as we went into the house. I could tell he wasn't happy.

"So what is there to do here?" he asked. "I didn't want to come, you know—Mom made me. Now I'm stuck here until the weekend."

"Yeah, I felt the same way, but it's not so bad," I said as I stopped at Bailey's room. "We can swim in the river and play in the hayloft—"

"And we found—" began Ollie.

"SHHH!" I said. I pulled him and Sofi into Bailey's room and Sal followed. "Can you just wait until I get my clothes changed?"

Ollie and Sal went through the bathroom to Brent's room, and I changed clothes as fast as I could. I hoped Ollie wouldn't spill the whole story, but when we got to their room, they were sitting on the floor, Ollie still in his wet swimsuit. He was waving around what looked like a big black plastic bug, except it only had four legs.

"Look what we found!" he cried, holding it up.

"What is it?" I asked.

"It's a drone," said Sal. "This is awesome!"

"What's it for?" I asked.

"You fly it with the remote control," said Sal. He was just as excited as Ollie. "My friend in New Jersey had a remote-control car, and he let me drive it."

"And it takes pictures," said Ollie. "Come on, let's go ask if we can fly it!"

Sal looked around the room and found an outlet. "Here, plug it in," he said. "The battery needs to be charged."

"Hang on," I said. "Did you tell Sal about the—?"

"No," said Ollie, "you told me to wait!"

He actually did what I told him? Amazing! We all went to the kitchen, where Aunt Abby, Uncle Jeff and Dad were eating some of Mrs. Martelli's biscotti. "Can we fly the drone?" asked Ollie as we grabbed cookies. He was practically a basket case.

"Where did you find a drone?" asked Dad. "Were

you snooping in Brent's room?" Ollie gave him a guilty look.

"It's an old one," said Uncle Jeff. "A little later, OK?"

"And weren't you supposed to put dry clothes on?" Dad asked Ollie.

We took more cookies and went out to the porch outside of Brent's room. It had a rail all the way around it and room for us all to sit.

"So what were you gonna tell me?" asked Sal.

Chapter 11
The Drone ~ *and* ~ The Underground Railroad Route

"**T**here's ghosts here!" said Ollie. "They smashed my space station and broke our pumpkin sticks!"

That got Sal's attention!

"WHOA!" he said. "Ghosts? Like more than one?"

"Well, we've only seen one," said Ollie, "a little girl, but there's another—"

"We don't know that!" I cut him off. "All we know *for sure* is there's this little girl who's always around, but we don't think she smashed the space station."

"Then who did?" Sal asked Ollie.

"There's another one, and he's done lots of bad stuff!" Ollie said.

"What else?" asked Sal. "Start at the beginning!"

So Ollie rattled off all the things that had happened since we got to the farm, starting with the falling hay bale, the hidden football, the rope, the wrecked Legos, the pumpkin sticks and the laughter, and getting pushed into the river.

"And I've seen eyes watching me in the trees, and a voice in the night told me to go away! I think it's 'cause I found an old watch in the cellar and the ghost doesn't want me to touch it."

"Back up!" said Sal. "How do you know this girl's a ghost? And why do you think there's another one? Maybe it *is* her doing the bad stuff."

"Because," said Ollie, "you can see through her, and she *glows*. And she doesn't have a reflection in the water!"

I finally had a chance to get a word in. "*I* don't think there's another one! The girl's a ghost for sure, but she seems to just follow us around. There's a real live guy here who I think wrecked the Legos and broke the pumpkin sticks."

Ollie jumped right back in. "I *know* there's another ghost, and he's mean—and you know what? I bet he let the chickens out last night!"

"So why would anybody do this stuff?" asked Sal. "That's kinda scary."

"Yeah, but the girl told me not to be afraid in my dream," said Ollie.

"She probably meant not to be afraid of Jeremiah," I said. "He's this guy who helps Uncle Jeff. He's always sneaking around and never talks, and I saw him put a Lego in the berry scale."

"But how could he make a rope go wild, or knock Ollie off the log?"

"Not you, too!" I said. "You think there's some invisible bully? Ollie's just a klutz, that's all!"

"What about somebody watching him from the trees?" asked Sal.

"I've never seen anybody!" I said. "But I saw Jeremiah put a Lego in the scale! And we saw him near the pumpkin patch—"

"You know what I think?" asked Sal. "You don't want there to be another ghost because *you* didn't find it."

"That's not true!" I said. "I saw the ghost girl just like he did, but there's not another one. The bad guy is that Jeremiah dude."

Sal put up his hand. "Why are you so sure? You're not always right, you know."

"Well, neither are you!" I shouted. He was making me mad and I wished he hadn't come to the farm.

"I'm gonna ask the Ouija board!" said Ollie.

The others hurried back to Bailey's room, but I stayed on the porch. Sal could be such a butthead! Back when we found Susie's ghost in my great-grandma's mirror, *he* was the one who didn't believe *me*. Plus, I was ticked at what he said, even though deep down, I knew maybe he was right. But I didn't want to be left out, so I counted to ten and followed them to Bailey's room. Ollie had his fingers on the Ouija board pointer.

"I've heard about these but I've never seen one before. What do you do?" asked Sal.

"Put your fingers on the pointer with mine," said Ollie.

"Go ahead," I said, "but it's all fake, anyway." I hoped it wouldn't work.

Ollie wasn't paying any attention. "Is there a mean ghost here at the farm?" he asked. Slowly, the pointer started to move. We watched as it wiggled up to the word "YES."

Ollie pumped his fist. "See?"

"Try this," said Sal. "Is it a girl?"

"What's so interesting?" Everyone jumped at the sound of Dad's voice. He and Uncle Jeff stood at the doorway. Uncle Jeff looked at the Ouija board and laughed.

"Bailey and her friends used to play with that all the time," he said. "Would you rather do that, or fly the drone?"

Ollie jumped up and grabbed the drone off the charger. We all followed Uncle Jeff through to Brent's room and out to the porch.

"Even though it's basically a toy, there are rules for

using it," said Uncle Jeff. "None of you are registered, so we have to keep it here on our property."

He said for now we had to keep it between the house and the barn where there weren't any trees. "You can take it out farther after you've had some practice, but don't fly it where you can't see it," he said. "And move it smoothly and carefully so you won't crash it."

Uncle Jeff showed us how to use the joysticks, then we all got to take a turn. It wasn't that easy. You had to think about left and right and up and down, and how fast it was going, and not let it crash. It was fun, though, especially seeing things from up above, like birds do!

"Let's plug it back in to recharge now," said Uncle Jeff. "You can practice some more tomorrow."

"Go wash your hands for dinner," said Dad.

As we crowded into the bathroom to wash up, Sal whispered, "So when can we see this ghost girl? And if there's another one, we're gonna find it!"

Dad stayed for dinner, and we told him about what we'd been doing at the farm. Aunt Abby asked Sal and Sofi about moving from New Jersey and how they liked living in Kansas.

"I've never been on a real farm before," said Sal.

"We're not real farmers, you know," said Uncle Jeff. "I teach high school history in Lawrence, and Abby teaches chemistry at Baker University a few miles down the road."

"We had history last year in school," I told Uncle Jeff. "I wrote a report on the Underground Railroad."

"Really? Did you know you're sitting right now near one of the main Underground Railroad routes in Kansas?" said Aunt Abby.

"For real?" said Sal. "Like, actually right *here*?"

"In Douglas County," she said. "Lawrence was a center of anti-slavery activity, and there were farms all around where fugitives could stop for help. They say at least 300 people, and maybe a lot more, came through here."

"One of the Underground Railroad stations—the Grover barn—is still standing," said Uncle Jeff. "We could go see it. It's not quite like it was back in the day, but the original stone walls are still there."

"Sweet!" said Ollie.

"The Underground Railroad took them west and north, away from Missouri, to keep away from the slave hunters along the border," added Aunt Abby.

"Yeah, we heard that people could be arrested just for helping slaves escape," said Sal. "That wasn't fair at all!"

"Well, it's true," said Uncle Jeff. "You know, there were big fights over whether Kansas would become a slave state or a free state. People killed each other over it."

"It was so important to some people in Boston—the Abolitionists—that they moved out here to help keep slavery out of Kansas," said Aunt Abby.

"As a matter of fact, several of the first real battles over slavery were here in Douglas County," said Uncle Jeff.

"Battles?" said Ollie. "Where?" He loves hearing about battles and wars and stuff.

"The Wakarusa War and the Battle of Black Jack were just a few miles from here," said Uncle Jeff. "We can go see the Black Jack battlefield, if you want."

Ollie was bouncing up and down in his chair. "Are there any ghosts around, of people who died in the battles?" he asked.

Uncle Jeff smiled. "Well, not that I've heard of, but they do say our barn is haunted."

Chapter 12

The Haunted Barn ~ *and* ~ The Ghost Has a Name

"**N**O!" I said. We stared at him with wide eyes. "The barn is haunted? Who's the ghost?" *Does Uncle Jeff know about this girl?*

"During the Civil War, some pro-slavers came and burned Lawrence," said Aunt Abby. "Have you heard of Quantrill's Raid?"

We shook our heads.

"Lawrence was a free-state town," said Uncle Jeff. "Quantrill and a gang of pro-slavery men rode in one morning and killed almost 200 men and boys. They burned most of the buildings, then rode around the county hunting down other free-staters. The story says they came to the cabin that was here and burned the old barn with some kids inside."

"*Kids*?" I said. "That's terrible!"

"So the kids' ghosts are in the barn?" asked Ollie. He was about to go bananas. "Have you ever seen them?"

"No," Uncle Jeff went on, "I've never seen a ghost." His eyes kind of twinkled, and I thought I heard laughter in his voice.

"But they *could* be there, couldn't they?" Ollie just couldn't give it up.

"We've never seen any evidence of ghosts," said Aunt Abby. "It's just an old story, nothing to be afraid of."

Well, that did it! You know how it is when grown-ups laugh at you, and think you don't know it? And they thought we were afraid of ghosts? I decided to play along.

"Cool! We can tell our friends we hung out in a haunted barn! Right, guys?" I laughed and gave Ollie the evil eye to make him shut up about it. The less said about ghosts, the better.

After Dad left, Uncle Jeff said, "Why don't you take Sal and Sofi out and show them how to take care of the chickens? Just remember to latch the door."

"Don't worry," I said.

On the way to the barn Ollie said, "I knew it! There's another ghost here for sure! Uncle Jeff said there were *kids* in the barn—not just one!"

"You have to admit, it all fits," said Sal.

"So what?" I said. "Even if there's another ghost, it's Jeremiah—"

"If you're so sure, why don't you just rat him out to your uncle or aunt?" said Sal. "They could make him stop. Then if stuff keeps happening, we'll know it's *not* Jeremiah."

I couldn't argue with that.

"I know I'm right," said Ollie. "I'm gonna fly the drone out over the pumpkin patch and see if anybody's messing with my pumpkin. Maybe I'll see the other ghost!"

When we got to the barn door, I said, "So the ghost girl was here last night when we came to feed the chickens. If we see her glow in the roost, we'll sneak in and catch her before she can get away!"

We tiptoed through the barn to the roost door, and saw the soft glowing light from inside.

"See the glow?" I whispered to Sal.

"Let's go!" he whispered back.

We opened the door as quietly as we could, slipped into the roost (being careful not to step in any poop), and crouched down so we could see under the nests. Bingo—there she was!

The little blond girl sat under the nests, playing with one of those fuzzy weeds that grew in the big field. I guess she was daydreaming and didn't hear us at first, but suddenly she looked up with a start. We crowded in close to keep her from getting away. Sofi smiled at the girl.

"I'm Sofi," she said. "What's your name?"

The little girl looked at all of us without smiling, but then said, "Katie."

"Katie who?" asked Sal. "Do you—did you used to live around here?"

She pointed toward the house. Right then Barker came nosing into the roost. Instead of barking at Katie, he just sniffed at her and went back out.

"You mean across the road?" I asked.

She shook her head, and said, "Right there." She was pointing straight at the house.

Sal leaned in a little closer and said, "So where do you live now?"

Katie looked down and didn't say anything. She looked so sad, I suddenly felt sorry for her.

"Katie, when did you live here?" I asked. "Who did you live with? Do you know the O'Briens, my uncle and aunt?"

Katie's lip quivered a little, but she looked up.

"We came when I was a baby," she said. Her voice was so soft, it was almost a whisper. "From Boston, but I don't remember it. I lived with Papa and Mama and Noah."

"Noah? Is that your brother?" I asked. Katie nodded.

"So," said Sal, "where are they now?"

"Papa and Mama are gone," said Katie, "but Noah stayed with me. He…he was with me in the fire."

The *fire*?! Did that mean what I thought it meant? As usual, Ollie cut to the chase. "You're dead, aren't you?" he asked.

Katie looked down and didn't answer for a minute, then she slowly nodded.

Everybody started asking questions all at once, even Sofi, but Katie just sat there looking at the ground.

"Quiet, everybody!" said Sal. "Let her tell us what happened to her."

Katie pulled at the fuzzy weed and then started talking. "We were in the barn and there was a fire. Noah tried to make me get outside, but I tried to save my chickens. Then I couldn't see or breathe, but I pushed the door open…and that's all I remember." Her little face looked totally miserable.

"So why are you following me?" asked Ollie.

Katie's head jerked up. "I have to go," she said. "Noah says so." In a flash she wiggled between Sofi and Ollie and disappeared through the door, leaving us staring at each other like zombies.

Ollie pumped his fist. "She has a brother! He's gotta be the bad ghost!"

"Well, I guess you got your proof," said Sal. "There's two ghosts for sure."

I nodded, but I was thinking of something else…

"OMG!" I said. "Did you notice? Barker? He didn't bark at her!"

"Holy moly, you're right!" said Ollie. "That means... Barker *knows* her!"

"Everybody act normal," said Sal as we went back to the house. We played some card games in the family room, and Aunt Abby asked us what we wanted to be when we grow up.

"Something with math, like a computer engineer," said Sal.

"I don't know," I said. "I want to travel all over the world."

"A gymnast," said Sofi.

"I'm gonna be a Ninja Warrior!" said Ollie. "The Ouija board said so!"

"Where do you want to go to college?" asked Uncle Jeff.

"Baker, where I teach, is a good school," said Aunt Abby.

Sal said he hadn't decided yet, but Ollie said, "I'm not going to college."

"Really?" I said. "Don't tell Mom and Dad that!"

"Ninja Warriors don't need college," he said.

"Most Ninja Warriors have a day job," said Uncle Jeff. "You like the drone so much, I thought you'd want to study robotics or artificial intelligence."

Ollie had that deer-in-the-headlights look. "I have a robot kit. Why do I need to go to college?" Is he clueless or what?

Uncle Jeff laughed. "There's a lot more to robotics than your toy kit!"

"You might change your mind in a few years," said Aunt Abby. "You have lots of time to think about what you want to do."

I kept fidgeting. I wanted to go talk about Katie. I mean, had she really been here since the Civil War? And why did she want us to see her? This was getting complicated!

I yawned and said, "We better catch some zzz's so we can be up early to pick blueberries!" The others all yawned, too. I was pretty sure Ollie and Sal were faking it (like me), but Sofi seemed really sleepy.

I led the way back to Bailey's room so we could decide what to do next, but before I even opened my mouth, Sal whispered, "Let's fly the drone again!"

Chapter 13
The Glowing Blobs ~ *and* ~ The Crash

What—fly the drone in the dark? Sal, the kid my mom gushes about because he's so perfect?

"Are you crazy?" I asked him. "It's almost dark and Uncle Jeff said—"

"Just for a few minutes," said Sal. "We'll be super careful."

"Let's take it to the pumpkin patch," said Ollie.

Uh-oh—the pumpkin patch was way past the barn, off-limits according to Uncle Jeff. I peeked down the hallway to make sure he and Aunt Abby were still in the family room. I hoped they wouldn't hear us.

"What if we lose it? Or crash it?" I asked.

"Don't worry so much!" said Sal. He seemed totally

sure of himself as he went through to Brent's room and took the drone off the charger.

"It's a straight line from here to the pumpkin patch," he said as we went out to the porch. "I'll bring it right back. Nothing can go wrong." We all watched him take it out toward the garden.

I was nervous about disobeying Uncle Jeff, and it was so dark by this time that the camera screen was a blurry gray. "Get it back," I said. "I can't even see it anymore!"

Sal worked at the remote, trying, I hoped, to get the drone headed back to the porch. Suddenly he whispered, "There's something out there!"

We crowded in to see. Sal was right—there was a fuzzy white shape at the edge of the dark screen, moving away from the pumpkin patch toward the trees.

"Look!" said Sofi. "Two white things!"

Sure enough, there were two separate white blobs on the screen, moving together. Ollie cried, "It's Katie, and Noah's with her!"

"They're going toward the trees," I said. "You can't go there!"

Sal didn't seem to hear me.

"I need to get it down a little," he said. "Just a little lower…" He tilted the control this way and that. "Oh, NO!"

"What?" I asked.

"I…I was trying to get it closer to the ground, and… and it went down!" said Sal.

Could this get any worse? Sal furiously twisted the joysticks, trying to get the drone back up in the air, but it was no use. "What're we gonna do now? It's too dark to go out and look for it!" Sal looked like he might cry.

We're busted for sure, I thought, but sometimes you just have to take charge, right? "Get inside and act like nothing's wrong."

Nobody spoke as we went back through to Bailey's room. We didn't even turn the light on, we just stared at each other in the glow from the night light.

"We'll look for it first thing tomorrow morning, when we go pick blueberries," I said. "It's probably right on top of one of the pumpkin vines." Maybe if I said it out loud, I could make it true.

"What'll we tell Uncle Jeff?" asked Ollie.

"Nothing!" I said. "Not yet, anyway. If we find it tomorrow, we won't have to say anything."

"And if we don't?" asked Sal.

I swallowed. Suddenly I felt like throwing up.

"Then I guess we have to tell," I said. "They'll find out anyway."

I was so upset at the thought of telling Uncle Jeff we'd lost the drone, I'd forgotten about the glowing blobs in the pumpkin patch, but Ollie pulled the Ouija board out

UNCLE JEFF'S FARM
→ → = RUNNING PATH
WAKARUSA
Water Fall Pool
Hollow Tree
Pumpkins
Blueberries
Alfalfa
Hay
Garden
Pump
Barn
Walnut Trees
Apple Trees
Cotton-Wood Tree
HOUSE
Alfalfa
Orion O'Brien

from under the bed. He and Sal put their fingers on the pointer.

"What's out in the pumpkin patch?" asked Ollie. The pointer kind of jerked around, then started toward the alphabet. After what seemed like forever, it stopped over the K.

"K—for Katie!" he cried. "The Ouija board really works!"

Sal pulled the pointer back to the middle of the board. "Will we find the drone?" he asked.

"Do you like it here in the dark?"

I whipped around at the sound of Aunt Abby's voice at the door. I hoped she hadn't been listening in. I had to think fast.

"We're just playing with the Ouija board," I answered.

"Yeah, it's fun in the dark," added Sal.

She probably thought we were crazy. "Well, remember," she laughed, "it's only a game. Aren't you about ready for bed?"

SOFI WENT RIGHT TO SLEEP AS SOON AS WE TURNED OUT THE LIGHT, but I laid awake for hours wondering (1) how we were going to find the drone and (2) if we didn't, what I would I tell Uncle Jeff. He'd know we disobeyed—what if he sent us home before we had a chance to figure out about the ghosts? Even worse, Mom and Dad would find out, too. Just when I'd started having fun, my vacation was turning into a disaster, and it was all Sal's fault!

But even though I was mad at Sal for losing the drone, I couldn't forget what he'd said earlier. Maybe I *did* always think I was right, with Ollie, anyway—after all, I'm two years older! But he was right about one thing: If it was Jeremiah who wrecked the Legos and the pumpkin sticks, I had to tell Uncle Jeff or Aunt Abby, and they would make him stop. Problem solved!

Except it wasn't, quite—I didn't want to tell on Jeremiah before we found the drone. And then I had another thought: what if the bad things kept happening? Now that we knew Katie had a brother, the pieces were falling into place. Ollie's idea about an invisible hand or whatever might not be so crazy after all. I felt bad for blowing him off.

And if Noah, not Jeremiah, was the bully? I had no clue how to deal with a mean ghost. Just thinking about it made me want to puke all over again.

Chapter 14

The Blueberry Haul ~ *and* ~ A Pumpkin Bites the Dust

I dawdled as I got dressed Wednesday morning. By the time I got to the kitchen, Sofi and the boys were already there, talking to Aunt Abby.

"Why don't you show Sal and Sofi how to gather the eggs?" asked Aunt Abby.

"Come on!" I said. I wanted to get out of the kitchen before anyone said something about the drone.

On the way to the barn Sal said, "Do you think we'll find it?"

"Sure!" I said. I was trying to sound confident. "The pumpkin patch isn't that big, and with all four of us looking, somebody's gotta see it."

When we got to the barn the chickens were all awake

(and the door was latched, so none of them got out). The chickens jumped to the floor to get the feed we put out, and Sofi wanted to pet them all. Sal went to a nest and picked up an egg.

"Hey, it's warm!" he cried.

"Well, duh, a chicken's been sitting on it," I said.

Sal looked out toward the worktable. "So, is that the dude you think is doing the bad stuff?" he asked.

"That's him—Jeremiah," I said. Jeremiah looked at us but didn't say anything, then climbed the ladder to the hayloft. As soon as he was out of sight, I whispered, "See how weird he acts?"

"When are you gonna tell your uncle what you think?" he asked.

"As soon as we find the drone!" I said.

"What are the chickens' names?" asked Sofi as we waited for the eggs to cook.

"Why don't you think up some names for them?" Aunt Abby suggested.

Sofi started ticking off names: "Henny-Penny, Fluffy, Daisy…"

After breakfast we asked Uncle Jeff for some more stakes so Sal and Sofi could pick out pumpkins. What we were *really* going to do, of course, was look for the drone.

I started looking as soon as we got to the patch.

Sal and Sofi picked out their pumpkins, then started searching, too. It was hard to keep track of where we'd looked because the vines went all over the place instead of in straight rows. The fuzzy leaves made our fingers and arms itch, but we couldn't stop. Finally, though, we gave up. It just wasn't there.

"I guess we have to tell," I said as I slammed the gate shut. I was still mad at Sal for taking the drone out without permission, and at myself for not stopping him—I'm the oldest, after all—and at Jeremiah, or Noah, or whoever was trying to ruin our fun time at the farm.

Uncle Jeff met us at the barn with sunscreen, water bottles and plastic pails, like the kind you get ice cream in. He gave Sofi a ride in the wheelbarrow all the way to the blueberry patch while Barker ran ahead.

"Wow!" said Sal. "How many bushes are there?"

"A hundred," said Uncle Jeff. "You should be able to get enough berries for dozens of pies." He picked a few berries. "Only pick the blue ones," he said. "If they're green or reddish, they're not ripe."

"Can we eat them?" asked Ollie.

"Sure," said Uncle Jeff. "Rinse the dust off with your water first."

We scattered out, looking for bushes with lots of ripe berries, and started filling our pails. I tried not to eat too many, but it was hard not to! As we filled our pails, we dumped them into the wheelbarrow and started again. I had a full pail ready to dump when I heard Ollie hollering.

"Look, you guys! Who did this?"

I hurried to where Ollie was standing by the wheelbarrow, which was turned on its side. Blueberries were all over the ground.

"Oh, no!" I cried. Sal and Sofi came to meet us.

"Why'd you dump the wheelbarrow?" asked Sal.

"I didn't!" cried Ollie. "I just came to empty my pail and there it was, just like this!"

I groaned. "OK, we've gotta pick them up." We set the wheelbarrow back up and used our pails to scoop up the blueberries.

"Psssst!"

I looked at Sal. "Isn't that Jeremiah over there in the pumpkins?" he said under his breath. I was on my knees picking up the last of the blueberries, but I saw the Royals baseball cap near the gate to the pumpkin patch. "Do you think he did this?" he asked.

"Well…" I started.

"It wasn't Jeremiah," said Ollie. "I bet it was—"

"I know what you think!" I said.

After we filled the wheelbarrow with blueberries, we took turns pushing it back to the barn to weigh them. Sofi almost tipped it over, but luckily Sal grabbed it just in time. She and Ollie kept sticking their blue tongues out, and eating more berries.

I wanted to laugh and join in the fun, but I was making myself sick worrying how to tell Uncle Jeff about the drone. I mean, I could have thrown Sal under the bus since he was the one who lost it, but somehow I thought Uncle Jeff would expect me to do the right thing.

Jeremiah wasn't in the barn when we got there, so we weighed the blueberries ourselves. We got over ten pounds! Uncle Jeff's truck was gone, so I didn't have to tell him about the drone…yet. We took the blueberries inside. Aunt Abby said we could take them to the cellar later to keep cool.

It wasn't quite time for lunch, so I said, "Let's go check the pumpkin patch again." I was hoping for a miracle—that the drone would somehow appear if we just looked a little harder. I also wondered what Jeremiah had been up to while we picked blueberries. Maybe he didn't spill the wheelbarrow, but did he do something else? We took off up the hill.

As soon as we got there, everyone checked their pumpkin stakes. I found mine, and Sal and Sofi did too. Ollie was pulling back the vines beside his stake, when I heard him shriek. He sounded like he was dying.

"My pumpkin!" Ollie shouted. He stood there

holding the long green pumpkin, which was broken off at the stem. Sal went and took it out of his hands.

"Will it still be OK?" asked Ollie.

"I don't think so," said Sal. "It can't get ripe if it's broken off."

Ollie's lip quivered a little. *Uh-oh,* I thought, *he can't take much more.* I put my arm around his shoulders and gave him a hug.

"I wanna go home," he whispered.

Chapter 15
Rescue #1 ~ *and* ~ A Clue in the Cellar

I know how you feel, I thought. I wanted to be any-where but here, so I wouldn't have to tell Uncle Jeff about the drone—but I felt sorry for Ollie. "It's OK, little bro," I said. "We'll find an even better one. Come on."

"Don't sweat it," said Sal, "there's hundreds more."

That seemed to make Ollie feel better. Before long he found another long, skinny green pumpkin he liked, and we moved the stake with his name on it to the new one. He wanted to keep the broken-off pumpkin, so he and Sofi took turns carrying it back to the barn.

"So, do you think Jeremiah did it?" asked Sal.

"Yeah, I do," I said. "We saw him right there!"

"Then what are you waiting for? You have to tell," he said.

I sighed. "I know, but then I'll have to tell them about the drone, too, and I just don't know…"

"Look, I'll tell them it was my idea, OK?" said Sal. "I'm really sorry…I didn't mean to get you in trouble for it."

"No, we're in it together," I said. "I should've stopped you."

Uncle Jeff was getting out of the pickup when we got back to the barn.

"Hey, kids, did you get enough blueberries?" he asked.

"Enough for lots of pies!" cried Sofi.

Ollie stood there holding his green pumpkin.

"What happened to your pumpkin?" asked Uncle Jeff.

"Oh, it got broken off," said Ollie. "But I found another one."

"That's kind of unusual," said Uncle Jeff, "but when the weather's this hot, sometimes they just fall off the vine. Shall we stack up the hay bales so you can get to the rafters in the hayloft?"

Ollie's face lit up. He put the pumpkin down and ran for the hayloft ladder with Sofi right behind him. All I wanted was to disappear. I dreaded hearing what Mom and Dad would say once the whole sorry story came out about the drone. Would I get grounded for a year? Get nothing for Christmas? Have to buy Brent a new drone with my allowance? I was imagining the worst when Sal grabbed my arm.

"Look!" he whispered, pulling me to the worktable. I almost fainted when I looked into the scale bowl.

There inside was the drone! It was dusty but otherwise OK.

My hands flew to my mouth—I'd been saved from a fate worse than death! Sal put his finger to his lips and we high-fived.

"Who do you think found it?" he asked.

"I don't know," I said, "but let's get it back to the house ASAP! They'll never know we lost it!" He grabbed the drone and sprinted toward the porch outside Brent's room.

A few minutes later we joined the others in the hayloft. Uncle Jeff had moved some hay bales into a pyramid that we could climb up to reach the rafters. Sal and I whispered the news about the drone to Ollie and Sofi. We were so happy we went a little crazy. I sprayed Sal's head with my water bottle.

"Boys against girls!" yelled Ollie as he sprayed me in the butt. Sofi sprayed Ollie in the face and Sal drenched my hair, but Sofi got him back by soaking his T-shirt.

Uncle Jeff put the last bale on top of the pyramid and jumped down. "It's pretty solid," he said, "but you better go one at a time."

It was perfect! Ollie climbed up first, swung across

the hayloft, turned around, and swung back to the pyramid to climb down.

"I'm a Ninja Warrior!" he yelled. Sal and Sofi climbed
up and swung across the barn. I felt so relieved that the
drone was back, I climbed up too. The hay stuck to our
wet clothes and we looked like scarecrows, but I didn't
care. "Thank you, Uncle Jeff!" I cried.

After Uncle Jeff left, we sat looking out the big doors.

"So who found the drone?" asked Ollie.

"Whoever did, we owe them big time," said Sal.

"Yeah," I said, "now I don't have to tell them we lost
it, but I still have to tell them about Jeremiah."

"And we have to make Noah stop picking on me,"
said Ollie.

"Well, after I tell on Jeremiah, the bad stuff might
stop," I said.

"It won't," said Ollie, "'cause it's not him!"

"I think Jeremiah found the drone," said Sofi.

"Seriously? Why do you think that?" I asked.

Sofi just shrugged. "I just do."

"Listen," said Sal as we headed back to the house,
"no matter what happens with Jeremiah, we have to find
out what's going on with these ghosts, right?"

I had to admit, it was good having someone else to
help us figure this out.

"Let's show them the watch," said Ollie.

The blueberries were sitting by the cellar door, so I pulled up the handle and we each grabbed a bucket. We were wet and dirty, and I shivered a little as we went down the steps.

"It's like a crypt," said Sal as he looked around. "So where's this watch?"

We set the buckets along one wall, then Ollie crawled under the steps and pulled the old bowl out. I took out the watch and flipped open the cover, then handed it to Sal.

"Wow, that's old-school," he said. He turned the button at the top of the watch. "It probably hasn't been wound in centuries." He held the watch out to Ollie. "Want to touch it?"

"Uh…OK." Ollie rubbed his hand on his shorts, then held it out to take the watch. As soon as it fell into his hand, he sucked in his breath.

"Does it hurt?" I asked.

"No, it just tingles, like before," he said. He held it up to his ear. "Hey!" he cried. "It's ticking!"

"Quiet, everybody!" I said. We all held our breath and listened, and sure enough, we heard a slow "tick… tick."

"The hand's moving!" said Sofi. She was right—the long hand moved with a little jerk.

Sal held the watch up to the light bulb. "See these swirls on the back?" he said. "It's fancy handwriting.

It looks like...a...j...w...h...e...e—it's a name! A. J. Wheeler!"

"So who's that?" asked Ollie.

Just then Aunt Abby called us for lunch. Ollie put the watch back in the bowl and shoved it back into the wall.

Chapter 16

Sabotage in the Hayloft ~ *and* ~ The Scoop on Jeremiah

Aunt Abby told us to go put on dry clothes before lunch, and when we got back to the kitchen, Uncle Jeff and Jeremiah were at the table. Jeremiah made me nervous, but I couldn't say anything with him sitting right there. Sal picked up the slack and asked Uncle Jeff to tell us more about the Underground Railroad in Douglas County.

"John Brown himself came through here," said Uncle Jeff.

"Who's that?" asked Ollie.

"One of the most famous Abolitionists before the Civil War. There's a giant painting of him in the state capitol. Have you seen it?" he asked.

Sal shook his head, but I remembered it. "You mean that one of a crazy-looking dude that takes up a whole wall?"

"That's the one," he said. "He wasn't crazy, just determined to help slaves find their way to freedom. He led some of them through Douglas County."

"Maybe there's ghosts of runaway slaves around here!" said Ollie.

Aunt Abby said, "You've got a thing with ghosts, don't you? Maybe we shouldn't have told you the rumors about the haunted barn. There's nothing to be afraid of, you know."

Uh, that's what you think…

"What were the kids' names who died in the fire?" asked Sal.

"I have no idea," said Uncle Jeff.

"My grandma might know," said Jeremiah. I perked up. It was the first time I'd heard his voice!

"Jeremiah's family has been in Douglas County since back in the 1800s," Aunt Abby told us. To him she said, "Why don't you ask her what she knows about it?"

AFTER LUNCH WE WENT TO SEE IF THE DRONE WAS FULLY CHARGED. It wasn't quite ready, so we went back to the barn. Jeremiah was in a back stall cutting wire off a bale of straw. He didn't look at us as we climbed the ladder to the hayloft. Ollie charged straight for the hay-bale pyramid. He was halfway up when I noticed one of the bales sticking out at a funny angle.

"Wait—" I started, but it was too late. The bales at the top of the pyramid came sliding down in a heap with Ollie on top of them.

"Whoa!" said Sal as he ran over to help. "That was like a hay avalanche! Are you OK?"

Ollie stood up and shook out his arms and legs. He was scratched up, but I didn't see any blood. "Somebody moved the hay bales!" he cried. "They didn't feel tight like they were this morning!"

"Maybe we climbed it too many times and loosened it up," said Sal.

We tried to fix the pyramid, but the bales were way too heavy for us.

Ollie sighed. "I'm tired of bad things happening to me!" he said. "I just wanna have fun at the farm, but every day it's something else!"

"Don't you see?" I said in a low voice. "Jeremiah was right downstairs when we came in! He's the only one who could have been up here after Uncle Jeff built the pyramid!"

"I thought you were gonna tell your aunt or uncle about him," said Sal.

"Well, he was sitting right at the table with us!" I said. "What could I say?"

"I still don't see why he would do it," said Sal. "Ollie—or any of us—could have gotten hurt!"

"He's just…twisted! Have you noticed how he never looks right at you?" I said. "Let's go to the river—I don't want him listening in."

Aunt Abby was in the kitchen when we went in the house to change into swimsuits. *It's now or never*, I decided.

"Aunt Abby, you know how some weird things have been happening to us? Like Ollie's Legos got smashed, and the sticks in the pumpkin patch got broken? Well, I think I know who did it."

"Really?" she said as she dried her hands on a towel. "And who do you think it is?"

"Jeremiah," I said as Ollie, Sofi and Sal came into the kitchen.

"Oh, I don't think so," said Aunt Abby.

"But he's the only one who's always around when bad things happen," I said. "And he acts weird! He never talks, and when I took the wheelbarrow in the barn yesterday, he was putting a Lego in the scale!"

"Did you actually see him do any of these things?" she asked.

"Uh…no," I said. "But—"

"Just listen," said Aunt Abby. "Jeremiah would never do that. It's true he doesn't say much. He has autism spectrum disorder. Do you know what that means?"

"I've heard of it," said Sal. "Isn't it, like, special ed? Can he read or anything?"

"Of course, he can!" said Aunt Abby. "He's very smart, but he doesn't always understand what people say and do, especially if they're sarcastic or joking. If he doesn't know you very well, he's afraid you'll make fun of something he says, so he just keeps quiet."

"Ohhh..." I said. "But I didn't know that—I just thought he was the only person who could have done everything!"

"I've never known him to do anything mean to anyone," said Aunt Abby. "But I'll talk to him."

"She's right," said Sal as we walked up the path toward the river. "We didn't *see* him do anything."

"Well, it proves *I'm* right!" said Ollie.

I almost wished I'd never come to the farm, so many things were going wrong. By the time we got to the river, I wanted to forget the ghosts and Jeremiah and have some fun. I'd brought a tennis ball with me and we took turns throwing it into the pool for Barker to chase.

"This water's so clear!" said Sal, standing in water up to his waist. "I can see everything on the bottom... hey, what's that?" He ducked into the water as Sofi and Ollie climbed onto the dead tree. I was ready to throw the ball, but stopped with my hand in midair when Sal's head came out of the water.

"Look at this!" he shouted.

Chapter 17

The REAL Bully ~ *and* ~ Setting the Trap

He was holding a red Lego block.

Ollie and Sofi shoved off the tree trunk and came over to see, treading water.

"Do you think it's one of yours?" asked Sal.

"Yes!" said Ollie.

We sloshed around to see if there were any more Legos in the pool, but we didn't find any. Then I had a thought.

"Do you feel like anybody's watching you right now?" I asked Ollie. He stood still a minute and shook his head.

"I don't think they're here now," he said. "And I don't hear anybody laughing."

"So where are they?" I asked.

"Come on," said Sal, "let's take the drone out and see if we can find them!"

UNCLE JEFF SAID WE COULD TAKE THE DRONE past the barn as long as we kept it away from the trees. We took it up to the hayloft doors, where we'd be able to see it anywhere on the farm.

"This'll be great!" cried Ollie. He took the drone out first, all the way to the sunflowers behind the blueberry patch, yelling, "I'm Top Gun!" Sal was watching the screen.

"Hold it right there," he said. "Somebody's up there under the trees."

Sal took the control from Ollie and lowered the drone a bit. Suddenly I saw a brown dress and yellow apron near the river path, partly hidden by the trees.

"It's Katie!" cried Ollie. "And somebody's with her!"

He was right. Someone wearing long brown pants and leather shoes stood next to Katie under a tree.

"It has to be Noah!" I cried.

"Let's go catch them before they get away!" Sal cried. He brought the drone back to the hayloft and we scrambled down the outside ladder.

I ran ahead, but by the time I pushed through the weeds at the edge of the trees, there was nobody there. When the others caught up, we searched along the sunflowers in both directions, but finally gave up.

"Dang, they got away!" said Sal. We turned to go back down the path.

"Ow!" cried Ollie. He was trailing behind the rest of us.

"What's up?" asked Sal.

"Something hit me in the back," said Ollie.

"Like what?" asked Sal.

"I don't know," he said. "It didn't really hurt."

After a few steps he cried out again. "Somebody's throwing things at me!"

When he turned around, a hard green ball hit him in the chest and bounced to the ground. "It's a walnut!" he cried.

I looked all along the trees but I couldn't see who was throwing the walnuts.

"You walk in front," said Sal. We lined up single file with Ollie in front and Sofi bringing up the rear, and headed back to the barn. No more walnuts came flying at us, but we heard a cackle of laughter. And it sounded mean.

BACK AT THE HOUSE, OLLIE TOOK THE DRONE INSIDE TO PLUG IT IN. The rest of us went to sit under the walnut trees.

"You don't still think Jeremiah's doing the bad stuff, do you?" asked Sal.

I sighed. "No, I guess Ollie was right all along," I

said. "It's that creepy Noah—he hid in the trees and threw walnuts at us! But what if he does something even worse? I can't just tell Uncle Jeff to make a ghost leave us alone!"

"I think if Noah wanted to do something *really* bad, he would've already done it," said Sal.

"What do you mean?" Ollie's voice startled me. I'd been so focused on Sal, I hadn't seen him come back from the house.

"Just what I said," said Sal. "Noah's a real bully, but he could have done a lot worse, you know. And I think Katie's watching out for you. Didn't she tell you not to be afraid in your dream?"

"Yeah," said Ollie.

"Oh, my gosh!" I said. "That's why she always shows up when something bad happens! She's making sure he doesn't get hurt!"

"Right," said Sal. "Noah's sending Ollie a message—"

"Yeah, I got it," said Ollie. "Loud and clear!"

"But Katie's trying to help!" cried Sofi.

"Now we just need to find out why he wants you to go away," said Sal.

"I'm not sure I want to know," said Ollie.

"Sure, you do," Sal went on, "and we're gonna make him tell us."

"Oh, yeah? How?" I asked.

"We'll set a trap," said Sal.

At dinner, Sal asked if he and Ollie could sleep outside on the porch that night. Aunt Abby said she'd get some sleeping bags for them. We met in Bailey's room to go over our plan.

"He knows we're looking for him," said Sal. "That's why he hid in the trees and threw the walnuts."

"He wants us to know he's there!" I said.

"So here's what we'll do," said Sal. "Ollie, you build something out of Legos in the hayloft, and we'll leave it there. Then we'll see if he takes the bait."

Katie wasn't in the barn when we fed and watered the chickens. Ollie took his box of Legos to the hayloft and built a gray flat thing with a platform at one end. He said it was an aircraft carrier. Sofi put Lego people and some little flags all over it and we left it near the doors. It was nearly dark when we got back to the house. Aunt Abby unrolled the sleeping bags on the porch and the boys brought out their pillows.

"If you want, you can leave a lamp on inside the room," she said. "Make sure this door's closed, but not locked, in case you need to come inside." After she left we sat on the porch, talking in the dark.

"I wonder where Katie was tonight?" said Sal. "I was hoping we could ask her why Noah's being so mean."

"She's there now," said Sofi.

I looked back at the barn. A dim light showed through the cracks in the walls.

Chapter 18
The Wild, Weird Night

I laid in my bunk in the dark, waiting for Uncle Jeff and Aunt Abby to go to bed. It was way past my bedtime, and I kept yawning, but I was so wired there was no way I'd fall asleep. I'd never been so nervous in my life. It was way worse than anything we'd been through with the ghosts of Samuel and Susie!

My mind raced with thoughts of all we'd discovered that day. My little brother had nailed it about the ghost. The falling hay bale…the rope swinging him…knocking him off the log…no human could have done those things. It had all been right in front of me, but I hadn't wanted to see it!

And that really bothered me: why had I been blindsided by the ghosts? I thought back to something Samuel

Grayhawk had said, about why he appeared only to kids. I squeezed my eyes shut and tried to remember…yes! Because they're more understanding and…and less fearful! That was it! Maybe grownups don't believe in ghosts because they're afraid to…what? To believe in something they can't see.

Was I getting too much like a grownup? I mean, I'm not even twelve! I made up my mind right then to not be afraid of things that seemed weird or impossible (after all, I'd already met two ghosts, even before Katie!). I couldn't believe how close I'd come to forgetting the important things I learned from Samuel and Susie.

But that wasn't all of it—why wasn't I in the loop about the ghosts from the very beginning? I have that special power to see them, don't I? I thought back. The first people to see Samuel were Sal and Ollie. Susie appeared in the mirror with me and Ollie. *Ollie.* He was—what do they call it?—the common denominator.

Ollie's the ghost magnet.

Suddenly the whole picture changed. If Ollie was the ghost magnet, what was I? But then I got it. I thought of all the things I'd learned from Samuel Grayhawk and Susie Chase. I'd promised to be a good sister. A mean ghost was after my brother, and it was my job to keep him safe. We'd just have to figure out what Noah wanted and make him stop.

I checked the time on my Amazon Fire…11:38,

almost midnight. I climbed down from the top bunk and woke Sofi up. We'd gone to bed with our clothes on, so all we had to do was put on our shoes.

We tiptoed through the bathroom to Brent's room and slipped out the door to the porch. I whispered, "Sal? Ollie? Are you ready?"

"Ready," said Sal. One by one, we climbed over the porch rail and crept toward the barn by the light of the yard lamp. I was so jumpy, I kept thinking someone was following us, but when I looked behind me, nobody was there. When we got to the barn we pulled the door open just a crack, so it wouldn't squeak, and slipped inside. A faint glow came from inside the roost.

"Should I turn the light on?" I whispered.

"No," said Sal, "it'll tip her off. Her glow makes enough light."

We crept over and sat by the chickens' door. We couldn't see Katie, but we knew she was sitting under the nests.

"Sofi, why don't you talk to her? You're not afraid, are you?" I whispered.

"No," said Sofi. She was huddled close to Sal, but sat up straight and said, "Katie? It's Sofi. Will you come see me?"

No answer. We waited and waited, hardly breathing. Sofi tried again. "Katie? We want to be your friends. Will you come and talk to us?"

Silence. I was afraid we'd have to give up and go back to bed when we heard a tiny voice say, "Here I am."

Right before our eyes, Katie appeared—at first just kind of a white outline in the dark, then slowly her face and clothes filled in.

She walked right through the wire door without opening it, and the white glow got stronger the closer she came. Maybe because it was so dark, or maybe I was just jittery, but watching her made me shiver! She stood a few feet away from us with a serious look on her face. I took some deep breaths.

"Katie!" I whispered. "Can you come over here and sit with us?" After a few seconds, she came closer but didn't sit.

"Where's your brother?" asked Ollie.

"Not now!" said Sal. To Katie he said, "We just want to know what you're doing here. We won't hurt you."

I wasn't sure she was ready to trust us, but she finally seemed to make up her mind and sat down a few feet away. "I like to be with the chickens," she said.

"So do I," said Sofi.

"I just wanted to get my chickens out of the barn so they wouldn't get burned up," she went on. "And then Noah told me to get out, but it was too late…I couldn't breathe anymore."

"If you're dead," asked Ollie, "why aren't you in a grave somewhere?"

"The river took us away," said Katie.

"The river…you mean in a flood?" asked Sal. Katie nodded.

"Uncle Jeff told us there used to be bad ones!" I said.

"So your ghost is still here, where you lived," said Ollie. "But why are you following me?"

"Because of Noah," she said. "I don't want him to—"

Sal cut her off. "Is Noah here? Right now?"

Katie nodded.

"Uh-oh," said Sal. That's when we heard a crash from up in the hayloft. It sounded like Ollie's aircraft carrier getting smashed up.

Katie looked up toward the hayloft. "Noah!" she called. "Please stop! They won't hurt us!"

Then we heard stomping and thrashing sounds. It sounded like someone was throwing bales of hay around the hayloft. That was it for me.

"We're out of here," I said, and grabbed Sofi's hand. I didn't even look to see if Katie disappeared or not. We hightailed it back to the porch as fast as we could and climbed over the rail, trying to not make any noise. We hunkered down behind the rail and watched the barn.

"Well, I guess our trap worked," said Sal.

"I hope Uncle Jeff and Aunt Abby don't wake up," I whispered. We didn't hear anyone from inside the house. Nothing seemed to be going on in the barn, either, and I was about ready to take Sofi back to Bailey's room when Ollie whispered, "Look!"

Two white, glowing figures came out of the barn door. One of them was Katie, followed by a taller one in long pants. There was no way to tell how old he was, but he looked about my height, so he was probably a little older than us. They moved up the path along the hay field. I didn't realize my heart was racing until they disappeared over the rise. We huddled behind the porch rail, hardly believing what we'd just seen.

"That really creeped me out!" I said. "Didn't the noise in the hayloft scare you?"

"Yeah," said Sal, "and I didn't wanna be there if Noah came down that ladder."

"I wasn't scared," said Ollie.

"Liar!" I said. "You ran back here just as fast as the rest of us!"

"So?" he said. "I wasn't staying there alone. But I don't think he was gonna come down the ladder. I think *he's* afraid of *us*."

"Why do you think that?" asked Sal.

"'Cause he could've been waiting there with Katie when we got to the barn, but he wasn't. He hid in the hayloft, and then he tried to scare us…just like he always does."

I thought about that. "You know, you're right. He never comes out where we can see him."

"It's like they say," said Sal. "Lots of times bullies are cowards."

"Well, the way he was throwing hay bales around," I said, "I think he was mad."

"I wonder where they went?" asked Sal. "They must stay somewhere by the river."

"Maybe to where their graves were, before they got washed away," said Ollie.

"We have to talk to Katie by herself!" I said.

"Let me know when you figure out how to do that," said Sal.

"OK," I said, and giggled. Then Ollie giggled too, and soon everyone was laughing, trying not to make any noise.

"Stop it—it's making my stomach hurt!" said Ollie.

"Shut up!" I whispered. "We'll wake up Aunt Abby!" Then I laughed some more. We were so tired, and so relieved to be safe back on the porch, we were slap-happy. "I've gotta get some sleep. I can't think straight! Come on, Sofi, we better get back to bed." I laughed again. I've had some weird nights in my life, but this one was the absolute weirdest yet.

Chapter 19

Another Dirty Trick ~ *and* ~ The Lego Trail

The next morning everybody slept late. Uncle Jeff had already gathered the eggs by the time we got to the kitchen.

"You must have slept well out on the porch," said Aunt Abby.

"Yeah…the fresh night air was really great," said Sal. I tried not to laugh.

"Do you still want to go see the Grover barn, the Underground Railroad station?" asked Uncle Jeff. "I have to go into Lawrence to pick up some books, so we can drive by there if you want."

"It's a good day to be in the car or inside," said Aunt Abby. "The weather forecast said it might be over 100 today. Why don't you go pick the ripe tomatoes before it gets too hot?"

"The good news is, our trap worked really well," said Sal after we left the house. "We got Noah to come to us. Now we just need to do it again."

"But not in the middle of the night!" I said. "That was just too scary!"

"And we need something different to use for bait," said Sal. "We can't just keep using Legos."

"The watch!" cried Ollie. "In my dream, he kept saying, 'don't touch it.' What else could he mean but the watch?"

"You mean, like leave it in the hayloft to see if he'll come after it?" I asked. "I don't know…."

"What if we just bring it with us? If he knows we have it, he might come and talk to us," said Ollie.

After we filled our basket with tomatoes, we hurried back to the barn to see what Noah had done to the hayloft the night before. Ollie ran ahead of us and went straight for the ladder. When he jumped onto the lowest step and reached for the rung above his head, the board pulled clean out of the wall. Ollie stumbled back.

"Hey!" he shouted. "The ladder broke!"

"Look, the nail's still sticking out of it," said Sal. "I bet Noah pulled it out after he came down from the hayloft last night."

"Let's try the outside ladder," I said. We ran to the

back of the barn and climbed up. Ollie led the way and pried the door open from the outside.

"Wow, he trashed the whole place!" he hollered as the rest of us climbed up. We tumbled into the hayloft and looked around. It was even worse than I'd pictured. Legos and bales of hay were scattered everywhere.

"How're we gonna explain this to Uncle Jeff?" I asked.

Nobody had an answer for that. We gathered up the Legos and put them back in the box.

"Where are the people?" asked Sofi. There were lots of blocks and flags, but no Lego people.

"Could that be what Noah wanted?" asked Ollie. "My Lego people?"

"Why didn't he just take them the first time?" I asked. "No, it's gotta be something else."

"Kids? Did you pick the tomatoes?" Uncle Jeff called from down below.

"We did!" I called back. We left the Legos where they were, hurried down the outside ladder and raced around to the barn door.

"Look what happened to the ladder!" shouted Ollie as soon as we got there. "This board pulled out when I tried to climb it!" He showed the board to Uncle Jeff.

"Huh," said Uncle Jeff. "That's never happened before." He got the hammer out of the toolbox and hammered the board back into place. "Just be real careful when you go up and down it. Take the tomatoes inside, and we'll go see Grover barn."

Ollie asked if we could ride in the back of the pickup truck, but Uncle Jeff said it's against the law. So we piled into the SUV.

"Is the Grover barn like your barn?" asked Sal on the way.

"Nope, it's made of stone," said Uncle Jeff. "They don't even use it as a barn anymore—the farm it was on got gobbled up by the city, and now it's a storage shed."

We drove into a neighborhood of big, nice houses, and right in the middle was a gigantic building made of brown and yellow rock.

"Most Underground Railroad stations are long gone," said Uncle Jeff, "and we don't even know for sure where they were, but there are written records telling about this one. John Brown led groups of slaves out of Missouri and they stopped here on their way north."

I touched the outside of the barn and tried to imagine running away in the night, knowing slave hunters were after me. What a terrifying thought!

Uncle Jeff picked up some books from the school where he teaches, then we went home for lunch. As soon as we finished, we told Aunt Abby we were going outside.

"It's awfully hot," she said. "Take your water bottles, and don't stay out too long."

OK," said Sal when we got outside, "let's follow the path they took last night."

We took Barker and went up the path by the hay-field. At the fork near the corner of the blueberry patch, Sofi called out, "Look!"

She was kneeling by the path, pulling back some blades of grass. There on the ground was a blue-and-red Lego figure.

"It's one of my men!" cried Ollie. He grabbed the figure and jumped up. "Maybe there's some more!"

We strung out along the path, crouching down to pull weeds and grass out of the way. Sal found a blue Lego man peeking out from the grass by the fence and another one in the dirt by the blueberry patch. Ollie and I each found one, and Sofi found another. We hurried to where the path led down the bank to the river. And there, right at the edge of the trees was a Lego astronaut!

"You know what?" said Sal. "It's like they were leaving a trail for us."

"It was Katie," said Sofi.

We stepped single file down the steep path to the river, looking on each side for more Lego men, but we didn't see any. We stood on the riverbank and looked around.

"It's weird how quiet it is," said Sal in a low voice.

He was right. The air was totally still and even the waterfall didn't seem to make any sound.

"I'm hot," said Ollie. "I'm gonna get in the water."

Chapter 20
The Message

"In your clothes?" I asked.

"I'll just get my feet wet," he said as he took off his shoes and socks and stepped into the clear water. Sofi did the same.

"Why not?" said Sal. "It *is* really hot."

Well, I wasn't going to stand on the bank and sweat while they were all in the water, so I took off my shoes and stepped in. It felt wonderful! I looked up through the trees that hung over the river and saw thick gray and white clouds. "It's weird that it's so hot," I said. "The sun's behind the clouds."

The water felt so good, it was only natural that we waded in deeper. We dipped our arms in, then our heads, and pretty soon we were all the way in the water.

Barker got in too, and we splashed and played tag and jumped off the log bridge. I told Sofi about the fossils I'd seen in the rock shelf and paddled over to show her. As soon as I got close enough to the rock to see it, the hair on the back of my neck stood up. I saw something that shouldn't have been there.

"Sal! Ollie! Get over here!" I shouted.

They paddled over to the rock to see what I was yelling about.

"What the—?" said Sal.

There in the sand at the edge of the shelf was a message written in big letters: "GO HOME."

Ollie looked shocked and maybe a little scared.

"This wasn't here yesterday," I said. "He had to write it after they came up here last night."

"Are they here now?" Sal asked Ollie.

Ollie looked all around. "Maybe," he said.

Sal jumped out onto the bank, picked up a stick and started hitting the bushes to see if anyone was hiding there. Sofi and I looked behind the log bridge and up by the waterfall, but we didn't find anyone.

Nobody felt like playing in the river after that. We started up the path, but before we'd gone two steps we heard a familiar sound: laughter. We all froze and listened. And I knew the laughter we heard wasn't Katie.

W ₑ went back to the hayloft so Ollie could gather up the Legos.

"Did you get the men all back?" I asked.

"No, there's still one gone," he said. "I guess it's just lost."

We sat on some hay bales and looked sadly at what used to be the hay pyramid.

"Noah's upping his game," said Sal. "He *really* wants us to leave."

"Well, he's making me mad!" I said. Seeing the words in the sand had ticked me off, and for the first time I really understood how Ollie was feeling.

"You know," said Sal, "that's what *he* is…Noah, I mean. Really *mad.*"

"Who does he think he is, telling us to go home?" I said. "He needs his butt kicked!"

"Well, if we're gonna do it, we have to do it soon," said Sal. "We have to go home in two days."

"And if we don't catch him before we go, he'll think he scared us away!" I said. "I'm not letting some bully get away with that!"

"I wish he'd just come right out and tell me why he wants me to leave!" said Ollie. He took his Lego box and water bottle and went down the ladder, and everybody followed. He got something out of the toolbox and sat down beside his green pumpkin.

"What are you doing?" I asked when I saw what he

had in his hand. It was a knife, and he was hacking at the pumpkin. "Don't cut your fingers off."

"It's not that sharp," he said. He cut mean-looking eyes and a frowning mouth into the pumpkin.

"That's pretty awful," I told him.

"So?" he answered. "That's what I feel like right now!" He set the pumpkin at the bottom of the ladder and laid the knife on the table.

Yeah, that's how we all feel, I thought.

It was so hot I thought the heat would dry us off, but we were as wet as ever when we went in the house. We tried to sneak past the kitchen, but Aunt Abby saw us.

"Would someone like to tell me what you've been doing?" she asked. Everybody looked at me. I couldn't think of a good excuse, so I just told the truth.

"Uh…we went to the river, and we were gonna just get our feet in, but it was so hot, we couldn't help it…sorry."

"You're awfully dirty," she said. "Go get changed and put those clothes in the laundry."

When we got back to the kitchen, Aunt Abby wasn't there.

"Quick!" I said to Ollie. "Go down to the cellar and get the watch!"

Sal pulled the cellar door open and Ollie hurried

down the steps. He came back a few minutes later and showed us the watch, then put it in his pocket.

"Storm's coming," said Aunt Abby as she came through the back door. "I put the chickens in and closed their door."

We went out to the barn. The air had a weird feel and the sky looked funny. The clouds were getting thicker and darker, but it was hotter than ever. We splashed our faces in the rain barrel to cool off. By the time Uncle Jeff came to get us for dinner, the wind was blowing real hard and the clouds were racing through the sky. Aunt Abby said it would be nice to get some rain, but she hoped it didn't bring a tornado.

"Could there be one?" asked Sal.

"It's possible," said Uncle Jeff. "Stay in the house after dinner. The chickens are already taken care of."

"If there's a tornado," said Aunt Abby, "we'll go to the cellar. Don't worry."

After dinner we went back out to the porch. It was still hot, but the wind had a cool feel. Even though it wasn't very late, it was almost dark outside.

"It'll suck if we never find out why Noah's so mad at us," I said. "I think Katie was about to tell us, right before he started tearing up the hayloft."

Ollie went inside and came out again a minute later. "My Legos are still in the barn," he said.

"I thought you brought them down from the hay-loft," I said.

"I did, but then I made the face on my pumpkin, and I guess I left them by the toolbox," he said.

The wind was picking up fast and it looked really stormy. "Uncle Jeff told us to stay in the house! You can get them tomorrow," I said.

"I want them now!" he whined. "I'll just run out there and get back real fast."

Chapter 21
Terror in the Barn

"**Y**ou're not going alone," I said, but Ollie was already climbing over the porch rail.

"It's just to the barn and back!" he cried. "I'm not a baby!"

"Cut the crap, you two," said Sal. "We can all go from out here, and they won't even know we're gone."

The trees were blowing like mad, with walnuts and acorns hitting the ground all over, but it wasn't raining yet and besides, we'd be right back. What could go wrong? We all climbed over the rail. As soon as we stepped away from the house we felt how *really* strong the wind was. It was hard to stand up straight, and I was afraid Sofi might get blown over. Leaves and twigs and dirt blew at our faces. We ran to the barn and slipped through the door, out of the wind.

It was super dark inside, but I found the light switch and turned on the floodlight above the barn door. Our shadows looked like monsters against the walls. That, plus the wind rattling the old wood, made it a little scary. Barker came out of one of the stalls, so we all felt better.

Ollie spotted his box of Legos under the table with his water bottle, right where he'd left them.

"Here they are," he said. "I put them down right by my—whoa! Look at my pumpkin!"

"What—?" I asked when I saw the horrified look on his face. Then I looked at the pumpkin. The knife Ollie had used to carve his pumpkin was sticking out of one of its eyes.

"Uh-oh," said Sal. "Looks like Noah's been here!"

We all looked wildly around the barn to see if anyone else was there.

"Listen for a minute," said Sal, "he might be up—" Suddenly a really loud CRACK made me jump. The barn shook with the thunder.

"That lightning sounded close!" I said. "We better go back!"

The others ran to the barn door while I went to turn off the light, but before I could there was another flash of lightning. Thunder rattled the barn again, and rain started pounding the roof.

Sal opened the door a crack, and we saw the barn-yard go from black to white and back. He shut the door to keep rain from blowing in, but water was starting to seep in under it. Then the barn light went out.

"Uh-oh," I said. I peeked at the house through the barn door and didn't see any light there, either. "I think the power's out."

"Should we run back to the house?" asked Ollie.

"It's not safe with this lightning," said Sal.

With the next bright flash I saw not just rain, but what looked like gigantic white marbles hitting the ground.

"That's the biggest hail I've ever seen!" I said.

"At least we're dry in here," said Sal. "We'll just have to wait it out."

The rain was coming even harder. At the next flash of lightning, we ran to the worktable and huddled under it in the dark.

"Do you think Aunt Abby will know we're out here?" I asked.

"Well, she'll know we're not in the house," said Sal.

"Just what I need," I moaned, "something else to get me in trouble."

Sal just shrugged. The lightning and thunder were close together now, and wind whipped through the cracks in the old barn walls. The hail hitting the roof was so loud we had to shout to hear each other. Maybe that's why at first I didn't hear the other noise—not lightning or thunder, but a CRE-E-A-K! CRE-E-A-K! above our heads. Something—or some*one*—was moving across the hayloft toward the ladder.

"Is it Noah?" asked Ollie.

"Oh, my God," I said. "What's he doing now?"

"I'm pretty sure we're gonna find out," said Sal.

"Oh, my God," I said again. I was too scared to say anything else. We huddled closer in the darkness. "We need to get out of here. Look what he did to that pumpkin!"

"What about the hail?" cried Sal.

I started to argue that it was better to get hit by hail than murdered by a ghost, when Sofi cut me off.

"Here's Katie."

Sure enough, in the pitch-black barn we saw Katie's glowing white shape coming toward us from the chickens' roost. She sat down beside us. Her glow made just enough light for us to see each other.

"Is Noah in the hayloft?" asked Sal.

Katie nodded.

"Can you help us?" asked Sal. "Can you tell him not to hurt us?"

Katie looked up toward the hayloft. "Noah won't hurt anybody," she said. "He just wants to scare you."

"Well, he's doing a good job!" I said.

"Why does he want to scare us?" asked Ollie.

"BECAUSE I WANT YOU TO GO AWAY!" The voice came from above our heads. Before anyone could move, we heard the creak of the hayloft floor again, and we looked up to see another glowing shape at the top of the ladder. I squeezed my eyes shut and hoped I was dreaming, but when I opened them, a boy about my size was stepping off the ladder, glaring at us. The stuffy heat from the afternoon was gone and the air in the barn made me shiver.

I was so terrified, I was afraid I'd wet my pants, but in a weird way, seeing him was better than hearing him stomp around in the hayloft. He wore old-looking brown pants with suspenders and a long-sleeved white shirt. His blond hair was cut funny and parted down the middle. Like Katie, he had dark smudges all over his hair and clothes, and his shirt looked like it had holes burned in it, with one sleeve almost completely gone. The white glow made it hard to tell, but I guessed he was about 13 or 14. The really scary thing about him was his icy blue eyes. They looked angry, but something else, too…I wasn't sure what.

"Why do you want us to go away?" asked Sal.

"Because I don't want you here!" Noah answered.

"That's not a reason," said Sal. "We're not bothering you."

"HE is!" Noah turned his angry stare on Ollie.

Instead of shrinking back or looking down, Ollie

stared right back. I couldn't believe how calm he was! Well, I couldn't let my little brother be braver than me, so I swallowed and said, "He's my brother and you better not hurt him! Why don't you pick on somebody your own size?"

Ollie's head whipped around. "You don't have to take care of me!" he yelled.

"Who are you anyway?" Noah shouted. "Katie, come away from those people!"

Katie didn't move from where she sat by Sofi. "They won't hurt us," she said. "You don't have to be afraid."

Chapter 22
The Phantoms

Her words rang a bell in my head. Could a ghost be afraid of *us*? I knew then what else I saw in Noah's eyes. Ollie had it right. It was fear. But what could he be afraid of?

Whatever, it made Noah angrier than ever. I didn't think the air could get any colder, but it did. He spoke to Katie.

"Why should I be afraid of him? I just want him to leave, but first he has to promise to keep his hands off things that do not belong to him!"

"You mean the watch?" asked Ollie. "I didn't know whose it was. I just wanted to see it."

"You had no right to touch it!" shouted Noah. "My sister and I never interfere in the lives of people here, so why did you summon us? You should learn to mind your own business!"

"Summon him? What's he talking about?" I whispered to Sal. He shrugged.

"But I didn't do anything!" cried Ollie.

Sal looked Noah in the eye. "What do you mean, he summoned you?" he asked. "You think he, like, cast a spell or something and made you appear? That's a lot of bull!"

"*You* know what I mean," said Noah, speaking again to Ollie. "You're one of *them*—those who commune with spirits. You came uninvited and stirred up all this trouble!" The glow around him got brighter the angrier he got.

"My aunt and uncle invited us," said Ollie. "*You're* the one who started picking on *me*."

Noah's angry eyes were the scariest thing I'd ever seen. It didn't help that the rain was pounding on the roof and the wind was howling. I put one arm around Ollie and the other around Sofi, who had her arms around Barker. I was ready to scream for help, hoping somebody at the house would hear me.

"Keep him talking," whispered Sal. "Maybe he'll tell us what Ollie did to bring him back."

Sal was right. If we could talk him down, maybe we could get him to leave us alone.

"You just admitted you're a spirit," I said. "But we've

seen spirits and ghosts before, and they weren't mean to us. They were nice!"

Noah looked at me and laughed that mean laugh we'd heard so many times. He said, "Silly girl, you think you understand ghosts and spirits? Well, I will teach you a lesson about interfering with a *phantom*!"

I didn't know what he had in mind, but it couldn't be good. I could tell Sal was as scared as I was. He leaned over and whispered, "Good, keep it up."

I tried not to panic. "You're the one who caused all the trouble! And anyway, what do you mean about communing with spirits or whatever you are? Why didn't you just tell us if we were bothering something of yours, like a civilized person?"

Noah laughed again, but Katie said, "Please, Noah! Tell them!"

"I think I get it," said Sal. "You and your sister live here…I mean, you're dead, but you're here, and the dog knows about you, but only certain people, like Ollie, can see you. Right?"

"And we can, too, when we're with him?" I asked.

"That's right," said Noah, stabbing a finger at us. "And I've had about enough of all of you! It's time for you to leave." He leaned a little closer and spoke directly to Ollie. "The question is, will it be your way or my way?"

"Noah, no!" cried Katie.

"Answer me!" he cried, ignoring her.

Ollie crossed his arms and said, "I'm not afraid of you."

I am, I thought, but kept my mouth shut to keep from screaming.

I swear Noah's eyes shot arrows at Ollie as he towered over him, and the ground under us began to shake. *Oh, no, on top of all this there's an earthquake?* I grabbed Sofi's hand and squeezed Ollie's arm just as Sal leaned in and whispered something to Ollie. Ollie sat up straighter and said, "That doesn't scare me."

The shaking stopped! Just like that! As for me, I was amazed to be still alive! I almost laughed, but then I looked at Noah again. He was angrier than ever. Katie said he only wanted to scare us, but he looked ready to kill Ollie. Noah's glow was so bright it lit up the barn. As I opened my mouth to scream, Ollie grabbed something from his pocket and held it up in front of Noah—the watch!

Noah staggered back like he'd been slapped. *Now's our chance,* I thought.

"Guys, let's get out of here now!" I cried.

But before any of us could move, Noah was back on his feet. There was something bright on the ground in front of him—a flame! It started small but got bigger by the second. Barker growled.

"Shall I remind you what happened in this barn?" asked Noah.

"He's going to burn us up!" I cried, ready to jump up and run out of the barn. Who cared about a little rain and hail and lightning? Sal whispered something to Ollie again.

"Noah, they didn't mean to bother us!" cried Katie. "Please stop!"

As sparks shot from the fire in front of us, a flash of lightning lit up the barn through the cracks in the wood.

After that everything happened so fast I could hardly keep track of it all. In the glare of the lightning, Ollie jumped up and squirted his water bottle on the flame in front of Noah.

As the flame sizzled and died, the light bulb flickered on, then off again, and in the dark I saw shock and surprise on Noah's face as the glow around him started to fade. Sofi whimpered and I realized I was squeezing her hand so hard it hurt. Sal was on his feet and ready to jump at Noah when the light came back on for good. Ollie and Katie stood in front of Noah, holding hands. The whitish glow around Noah was almost gone, and he looked like just a kid in dirty, old-fashioned clothes. He dropped to his knees and looked at them.

"You...you're not afraid?" he said to Ollie.

"I'm not," said Ollie, but I heard a little quiver in his voice.

"Katie?" said Noah. "I just didn't want...."

Katie let go of Ollie's hand and went over to her brother. "It's time to stop," she said, and put her arms around his shoulders. "Just tell them…they don't mean any harm."

I must have been in shock because I sat there gawking at the whole scene. When I came to my senses, Noah was kneeling on the ground with the rest of us all around him. His shoulders shook, and he rubbed at his eyes.

"Noah?" said Ollie. "I'm going home on Saturday. What do you need to tell me?"

Noah looked like a completely different person now—not angry, not glaring, not even afraid, just… *tired*. And I realized it probably took all the energy he had to make the ground shake and the flame light up. He and Katie had both lost most of their glow and were fading away like smoke.

Something else was different, too—it was *quiet*. The rain sounded softer, and the wind wasn't howling any more. The thunder seemed to be moving away.

"Orion? Sal? Are you in there?" Uncle Jeff's voice startled us as he opened the barn door.

Chapter 23
Safe and Sound ~ *and* ~ Phantoms Explained

A moment later Uncle Jeff was inside, wearing a raincoat and hood and carrying an armful of towels. We all jumped up.

"You kids gave us a scare!" he said. "When the rain started, we went to get you and take you to the cellar, but we couldn't find you! What in the world were you doing?"

I ran and threw my arms around Uncle Jeff. "I'm so glad to see you!"

"Aunt Abby was worried sick, but I saw the light on in the barn before the power went out," he said, "so I figured you were out here. Is everybody OK?"

WE ALL FOLLOWED UNCLE JEFF BACK TO THE HOUSE.
Even though the rain had almost stopped, we were wet
and cold by the time we got there. Aunt Abby ordered us
to go take showers. After I was clean and dry, I peeked
into Brent's room. Ollie was bouncing around in his
underwear.

"Ollie! Get some shorts on!" I said.

"They're in the laundry," he said.

"What? How many pairs did you bring?"

"Uh…two?" he said. I slapped my forehead.
Sometimes I think there's no hope for him.

"Here," said Sal, throwing him a pair of black gym
shorts. Ollie put them on and danced from foot to foot
like a maniac.

"Get your act together or Aunt Abby will ask what's
wrong with you!" I said.

"Well, wait'll you hear—" he started, but stopped
when Uncle Jeff came to the door.

"Later!" whispered Sal.

UNCLE JEFF HERDED US TO THE FAMILY ROOM, where
Aunt Abby fussed over Ollie and Sofi and made them sit
beside her on the couch. We told them we were fine and
that we'd just waited in the barn for the storm to pass. I
won't lie, though, it felt great sitting there warm and dry
with the light on!

"Now," said Uncle Jeff, leaning forward, "you weren't

even out there fifteen minutes, and it looks like you're all OK, but going to the barn was a bad idea. I told you to stay in the house because a storm was coming. What were you thinking?"

"I'm sorry, Uncle Jeff," I said, "but Ollie left his Legos out there and wanted to go get them, and I wouldn't let him go alone."

Ollie rolled his eyes at me but said, "Yeah, it was my idea. I guess it was pretty dumb."

"I was ready to come after you when the hail started," said Uncle Jeff, "but I waited until the worst of it was over. I hope you weren't too scared."

We all looked at each other. *We were terrified, but not of the storm*!

"Barker was with us," said Sofi.

"Are you gonna tell Mom and Dad?" I asked.

"I think you should tell them," said Aunt Abby. "It was a really bad storm, so it'll be on the news. They'll want to know you're all OK."

"Right," said Uncle Jeff. "The lightning came close—I'm pretty sure it hit the cottonwood tree."

"You mean that real tall one with the shimmery leaves?" I asked.

"That's the one," he said.

"Well, now that you're all safe and sound," said Aunt Abby, "who'd like some popcorn?"

"ME!" we all shouted. So we munched our popcorn

while Uncle Jeff turned on the television to see reports of the storm. He said we wouldn't know how bad it was until tomorrow.

"Anybody feel like kicking back and watching a movie?" he asked.

"I do!" I said, and Sofi clapped her hands. Normally Ollie would have been elbowing everyone out of the way so he could pick out the movie, but he looked at Sal and said, "We were just gonna hang out in the bedroom awhile."

"Woo-hoo!" I shouted. "Girls get to pick!" I high-fived Sofi as Sal and Ollie headed for the hallway.

"Hey, you were gonna help me look something up," said Sal. He jerked his head toward the bedroom and gave me a funny look. "Remember?"

"Oh…right," I said. "Come on, Sofi. I promised."

"You're probably all pretty worn out," said Aunt Abby. "We'll save the movie for tomorrow night."

"This better be good," I muttered as we trooped down the hallway.

"Get in here quick," said Sal as he ducked into Bailey's room. "Ollie's got something to tell you that you won't believe!"

All four of us crowded onto the lower bunk to wait for Ollie's bombshell.

"You know when Katie was holding my hand?" he said. "Right after I squirted the water on the fire?"

"Yeah, yeah, so?" I asked.

"Well…I couldn't feel her hand," he said.

"You mean like your hands were too cold or something?" I asked.

"No! I couldn't *feel* her hand—it's like it wasn't really there! Now do you get it?"

I gasped. What could that mean? Her hand wasn't really there? Were we all crazy?

"It must have something to do with what they are," said Sal. "What was that word—fantem?"

I grabbed the Amazon Fire and typed in "what is a fantem." The hits that came up spelled it "p-h-a-n-t-o-m." I read the definition.

"It says a phantom is something 'without material substance,'" I read. "Like a dream or a mirage."

"Like when people think they see water in the desert!" said Sal. "But it's not there!"

"What?" asked Ollie. "So we see Noah and Katie, but they're not—"

"Not really there!" I finished.

"I guess that's why you didn't see Katie's reflection in the water," said Sal.

"O-oh," said Ollie. "And it's why I couldn't feel her hand!"

"But they have some kind of energy," said Sal, "'cause look at all the stuff Noah did!"

"Holy smokes," I said, "I thought I understood

ghosts, and spirits, but now I'm more confused than ever!"

"Well," said Sal, "I guess there's different kinds of ghosts. Samuel was different from Susie, so why shouldn't Katie and Noah be different, too? I mean, the only thing the same about them is they're all dead."

"We're all different when we're alive," said Ollie, "so why shouldn't we be different when we're dead?"

"I never thought of it that way," I said. "Anyway, you were the hero tonight! I mean, you said you weren't scared when Noah made the fire, but you're such a liar!"

"Well, yeah," grinned Ollie, "but I wasn't gonna let Noah know it."

"That's my man!" said Sal, slapping him on the back.

"You were awesome!" said Sofi.

"Well, I remembered how Samuel stood up to those big kids at Halloween," he said. "He told us he had to do the right thing even if he was afraid. And then when the ground stopped shaking, Sal told me he thought Noah was losing his energy."

"But it was still amazing how you put out the fire!" I said.

"Sal whispered to me to get the water bottle," said Ollie. "So I just jumped up and squirted it on the fire."

"I think he started to lose his energy when you told him you weren't afraid," said Sal. "He wasn't expecting that."

"I'm really proud of you!" I said.

"You are?" He sounded surprised.

I ruffled his hair. "Of course, I am!" I said. "But I'm pretty bummed that we still don't know what Katie wanted him to tell us, and why he's so angry. What if we never find out now?"

"Oops, I almost forgot," said Ollie. "Katie told me to come to the river tomorrow."

Chapter 24
After the Storm ~ *and* ~ A Clue About Noah

When I turned out the light that night I wasn't sure I'd ever get to sleep, but the next thing I knew, Aunt Abby was telling me it was time to get up. I looked down and saw Sofi already putting her shoes on. I must have slept like a log! Then I remembered the night before.

I got dressed and went down the hall. When I passed the family room, the television news was on, showing pictures of torn-up buildings and trees down on the ground. *Did that happen last night?* In the kitchen, Uncle Jeff was sitting at the table with Jeremiah, who was talking again!

"There are trees down along the road to Baldwin," he said, "and the Jamisons' barn got hit. There's almost nothing left."

"It was a twister for sure," said Uncle Jeff. "We got lucky it went south of us."

Sal and Ollie came into the kitchen. "A twister?" asked Sal. "You mean a tornado?"

"That's right," said Uncle Jeff. "It did some real damage to our neighbors' barn, but there were no injuries."

Jeremiah showed us photos on his phone of what used to be a barn. It was just a pile of boards. There was also one of a big tree pulled up by its roots.

"The tornado tore that barn apart?" asked Ollie. "Awesome!"

Uncle Jeff shook his head. "It's just lucky the house wasn't hit," he said.

"Whoa!" said Sal. "I can't believe a tornado is that strong!"

Aunt Abby put plates of French toast in front of us, which we scarfed down like we were starving.

"By the way," said Uncle Jeff, "your dad texted last night to see if we got hit by the storm. I told him we were all OK, but I'm sure he'll want to hear about it from you."

"I can't wait to tell Mom and Dad!" said Sal. "And Josh and Alex, too! Can we go see where it hit?"

"Maybe later," said Uncle Jeff. "I need you to stay here and help Aunt Abby clean up while we go help the Jamisons. She'll bring you over later to see the damage."

AFTER BREAKFAST WE WENT OUTSIDE. The clouds were breaking up and it was a lot cooler than the day before. The yard was full of leaves and twigs and a few big branches, and there were apples and green walnuts on the ground under the trees. Aunt Abby stood looking at a long streak going down the side of the cottonwood tree where the bark was burned off.

"I'm glad the lightning hit the tree instead of the house or the barn," she said, "but I hope the tree will survive."

Uncle Jeff and Jeremiah left in the truck, and we helped Aunt Abby pile up all the sticks and leaves from the yard. We loaded them in the wheelbarrow and dumped them in a ditch behind the pumpkin patch. We checked on our pumpkins while we were there, and they didn't seem to be damaged.

"When are we going to the river?" asked Ollie. "We have to meet Noah and Katie today!"

"The river!" I said. "I wonder what all that rain did to it?"

We ran around the blueberry patch toward the path that led to the river. Before we even got to the trees, we heard rushing water.

"Listen to it!" said Sal.

We didn't have to go far down the path to see how high the water was. It was running along through the trees halfway up the steep bank.

"Let's go on down," said Sal.

"No way!" I said. "What if you slip and fall in or something? You almost got me in trouble when you took the drone out at night, but you're not doing it now! If you go down there, I'm gonna go get Aunt Abby!"

"Oh, all right," said Sal. "I just wanted to take a peek."

"But we have to go there!" cried Ollie. "I promised Katie!"

"What if they fell in?" asked Sofi. She sounded worried.

"They're already dead, so I don't think this can hurt them," said Sal.

"Look, we can't go down there now," I said. "Maybe the water will go back down after a while. Come on, Aunt Abby's waiting to take us to see where the tornado hit."

IF YOU'VE NEVER SEEN WHAT A TORNADO CAN DO UP CLOSE, it's unreal—not just the damage, but how it can totally destroy some things and not even touch others! We ooh-ed and aah-ed as we drove to the Jamisons' and saw broken trees and pieces of buildings scattered in the fields.

"It's like a giant smashed the barn!" Sal shouted as we pulled up to the house. Mrs. Jamison came to meet us and pointed out the crooked path where the tornado had ripped through the farm.

I couldn't take my eyes off the barn. The only thing still standing was part of one wall. I shuddered—what if the tornado had hit Uncle Jeff's barn while we were there with Noah and Katie?

A lot of neighbors were helping with the clean-up. Aunt Abby had brought sandwiches, and we passed out food and water to everyone. Uncle Jeff was sitting on the back of the pickup with Jeremiah and another guy.

"Kids, this is Jordan, Jeremiah's brother," said Uncle Jeff. "Remember when you asked about the family who lived on our farm during Quantrill's raid, when the barn burned? Jordan can tell you."

"Hi, guys" said Jordan. He looked a lot like Jeremiah, but was real friendly and talkative. "Yeah, Jeremiah asked our grandma what she knew about the fire in the barn. She's been hearing stories about it all her life. She said the day Quantrill burned Lawrence, some of the gang came to your farm. They kidnapped the farmer and set the barn on fire, with two kids, a boy and a girl, inside. Their dad was killed that day, and their mother took the baby and moved up to Topeka."

"Did she know the kids' names?" I asked.

"No," said Jordan, "just the family name—Wheeler."

"The kids liked hearing the haunted barn story,"

said Uncle Jeff. "Tell your grandma thanks for the information."

"Yeah, thanks," we all said. Nobody said anything about the name on the watch.

After everyone had eaten lunch, Uncle Jeff said, "I'm ready for a break. If you want to see the battlefield I told you about before you go home tomorrow, we're halfway there. What do you say?"

I knew Ollie was worried about how we would find Noah and Katie, but seeing a battlefield was his idea of heaven. He and Sal high-fived, and we all piled into the SUV. Aunt Abby took Jeremiah back to the farm in the truck.

Chapter 25
The Black Jack Battlefield ~ *and* ~ Rescue #2

I almost didn't see the sign that said "Black Jack Battlefield and Nature Park," it was so hidden by the trees. We pulled off the gravel road and parked in front of a big white house. There was a pump out front, like the one at Uncle Jeff's, and a sign with information about the battle.

"I wanna see where the soldiers fought!" shouted Ollie.

Behind the house was a big yard with trees all around.

"We don't know the exact spot, but somewhere in this clearing is where the battle took place," said Uncle Jeff.

"So who won?" asked Sal. "The North or the South?"

"It wasn't a battle between the two armies," said Uncle Jeff. "It was in 1856, before the Civil War even started. This was guerilla warfare."

Ollie snorted. "Gorilla warfare? They fought with gorillas?" He danced around and scratched his ribs.

Uncle Jeff laughed. "Not gorillas, like the animals," he said. "G-u-e-r-i-l-l-a. It means they weren't members of an army, wearing uniforms, they were just regular people fighting for what they believed in. Remember John Brown, who led so many slaves to freedom on the Underground Railroad? He and his followers fought several battles around here. And Quantrill's gang, the ones who burned Lawrence, were guerillas, too."

He led us to the trees that wrapped around the field, to a creek with water rushing through it. "The pro-slavery men would have camped here to get water for their horses. John Brown and his men attacked them as they slept, before the sun was even up."

"Did he win?" asked Ollie.

"He did," said Uncle Jeff. "The free-state men were outnumbered, but they managed to get the pro-slavers to surrender."

"But why here?" asked Sal. "Why did they fight over an empty field?"

"Missouri's just a few miles away," said Uncle Jeff. "In the Border War a lot of pro-slavers came from there to try and make Kansas a slave state. Who knows what our country would be like now if they'd succeeded?"

"Did anybody get killed?" asked Ollie.

"Not here at Black Jack," said Uncle Jeff, "but many people were killed in other battles. That's why they called it 'Bleeding Kansas.'"

We all nodded. "Yeah, we know," said Sal.

"You know, John Brown might have stood right where you're standing now," Uncle Jeff went on. "Think about it…it's daybreak…the pro-slavers are asleep by the creek as the free-state men sneak up…then the hollering and shooting start."

"Yes! I'm a guerilla!" cried Ollie. He dived into the grass and pretended to shoot a rifle.

Listening to Uncle Jeff, I could really imagine it. "Wow," I said, "this is a *lot* better than reading about it in a book."

I decided he must be a great teacher.

"So, was Quantrill's raid part of this battle?" asked Sal as we walked back to the SUV. "When they burned Lawrence, and the barn with the kids inside?"

"No, that was several years later, after the Civil War was in full swing," said Uncle Jeff. "Kansas was a free state by then, but there was still a lot of violence along the Missouri border."

"But why would anybody kill kids?" I asked.

"They probably didn't know the kids were in the barn," said Uncle Jeff. "Quantrill didn't usually hurt women or young children, but I've heard he ordered his gang to kill every boy tall enough to hold a rifle."

I sucked in my breath. Nobody said anything as we got into the SUV, but I knew what we were all thinking: *Noah's tall enough.*

As soon as we got back to the farm, Sal said, "What are we gonna tell your uncle about the hay pyramid? Should we say we did it?"

I sighed. With everything else going on, I'd forgotten about the wrecked hay pyramid. "He'd never believe that. Maybe he'll think the tornado knocked it down. We can't exactly tell him a ghost—I mean a phantom—did it!"

"There's gotta be a way we can fix it," said Ollie. He raced up the ladder to the hayloft and we all followed. "What if we—" he started, then stopped short. "Holy CRAP!" he shouted, then clamped both hands over his mouth.

I busted out laughing at the look on his face, and said, "Don't worry, I won't tell Mom!"

Then I saw the pyramid. The bales were perfectly stacked up, just like the day Uncle Jeff built it!

Sal walked slowly around the pyramid. "Somebody did us a BIG favor!"

"But who?" I asked.

"Who cares?" yelled Ollie as he ran for the hay pyramid. We all climbed to the top and swung across the hayloft. It was fun, but I couldn't forget what Uncle Jeff had said. I sat down on a hay bale, and the others came and sat too.

"Remember what Uncle Jeff said, about the boys tall enough to hold a rifle?" I asked. "You know what that means, don't you?"

"Yeah…Noah was gonna get it either way," said Sal.

"What do you mean?" asked Ollie. Then I saw the wheels turning in his head. "*Oh*…either he got killed in the fire, or killed by the bad guys. That sucks!"

"No kidding," said Sal. "He never had a chance."

"We *have* to find them before we leave!" I said.

Back at the house, Aunt Abby was canning dill pickles—I could tell by the smell—and I decided it was a good time to try and make up somehow for what I'd said about Jeremiah.

"You know when I said I thought Jeremiah wrecked Ollie's Legos, and broke our pumpkin sticks?" I asked her. "I don't think it was him anymore. I'm real sorry. I hope I didn't get him in trouble."

"He's not in trouble," said Aunt Abby. "I haven't even talked to him about it. I was here in the kitchen while you were at the battlefield." She was lining up jars on the counter. "Jeremiah was busy in the barn with something."

"He was?" I asked. I looked at Sal, then Ollie, but neither of them said anything.

"I'm really glad you changed your mind about him," said Aunt Abby. "He's not the kind of person who would do anything mean, especially to younger kids."

"Uh, well, I know that now," I said. "So you don't have to say anything to him. Please?"

Aunt Abby smiled. "Of course, I won't."

Girl, you have just been saved again!

Chapter 26
The Hideout

We hurried down the hall to Brent's room. Ollie was about to go crazy.

"Jeremiah fixed the hay pyramid!" he cried.

"And it's not the first time he bailed us out," said Sal. "Remember when we picked blueberries, and he was in the pumpkin patch?" I nodded. "And then after we weighed our blueberries, the drone was in the scale?"

I slapped my forehead. "Oh, my God! Jeremiah found the drone! That's what he was doing in the pumpkin patch!"

"I *knew* he didn't do anything bad to us," said Ollie.

"You were right," I said. I could just hear Dad's voice: *if you knew then what you know now….* "I feel awful. I wish there was a way we could make it up to him."

"We'll just be nice to him," said Sofi.

"You always know what to do," I said, and pulled her ponytail.

"Anyway," said Ollie, "we have to find Noah and Katie! We don't have much more time!"

"Maybe we can find them with the drone," said Sal. He unplugged it and took it out to the porch. Before long it was in the air and out over the garden.

"Remember, don't go past the trees," I said.

"I know, I know," he said. "But they might be waiting for us somewhere."

Sal hovered the drone over the pumpkin patch, then the blueberry patch, the hayfield and the alfalfa field, but there was no sign of them. As the battery began to run down, he made one last loop along the sunflowers. When the drone got to the river path, his head jerked up.

"There they are!" he said.

We crowded around the screen. There, at the edge of the trees, was Katie's white-blond hair. Sal dropped the control and we jumped over the rail and headed for the path.

Barker bounded out of the barn and ran with us. As we pushed through the sunflowers, Ollie started calling, "Katie! Katie, we're here!"

We stopped and looked around, but they were nowhere in sight. I ran along the trees in one direction and Sal ran in the other, searching in the bushes and vines.

"They were right here!" I said as I ran back to meet Sal. "Do you think they ghosted us?"

Sal gave me a look and said, "Ha, ha." That's when I realized Ollie and Sofi were gone.

Uh-oh! Did they slide down the bank and into the water? I could hear the river rushing below us, and almost had a panic attack.

"Pssst! Orion!"

It was Ollie's voice—what a relief! I crouched down to look into the underbrush and saw two dark brown eyes behind the leaves. And there was Barker's nose! I motioned to Sal and we ducked into the bushes.

We crawled on our hands and knees in a row—Barker first, then Ollie, me and Sal—deeper into the trees. The shade was so thick, it was almost dark, and twigs and sharp leaves scratched at our faces. I was looking at the ground to make sure I didn't put my hands on anything sharp when my head collided with Ollie's butt.

He was stopped in front of a big, hollowed-out dead tree trunk. Thick vines twisted all around it, and it was surrounded by tall trees that shut out the sunlight. It was the perfect hideout, dark and quiet. We could have been a million miles from the farm.

Noah, Katie and Sofi sat inside the tree trunk. The white glow surrounded them all—even Sofi—and for a second I was afraid they'd turned her into a phantom! I started to pull her away, but Noah put his hand up to stop me.

"Don't be afraid," he said. "She's not in any danger. Katie insisted that we see you again today. She wants me to…to apologize for the things I did to you."

I looked all around me. "Is this where you live…I mean, where you—?"

"It is near where we were buried," said Noah.

What could I say to that? I changed the subject. "We never would've known you were here, you know," I said. "I mean, here at the farm."

"And that is how I wanted it," said Noah, "but the black-haired boy sensed that I was here, and then he discovered the watch. I was angry and afraid that my secret would be found out."

Ollie took the watch out of his pocket. "This is a secret?" he asked. "It's just an old watch I found in the cellar! Why do you even care?"

He held the watch out to Noah, but Noah didn't take it. He just looked away.

"Tell you what," I said, "we'll go first and tell you about us, then if you want, you can tell us your secret." I took a deep breath. "I'm Orion, and Ollie's my little brother. We came to stay with our aunt and uncle for a few days before school starts. Then our friends

here"—I pointed to Sal and Sofi—"came to help us pick blueberries."

Noah looked at me closely. "You go to school?" he asked.

"Uh, yeah," I said. "Anyway, when we got here, things started happening to my brother—"

"And we went to the cellar and I knew there was something there," interrupted Ollie. "And I found the watch."

"So at first we thought this neighbor guy was picking on us, but Ollie thought it was a ghost," I added. Watching Noah, I realized he wasn't so much older than me—maybe twelve or thirteen. He looked a lot younger when he wasn't angry.

"Then Orion's uncle told us the barn was haunted by some kids who died in a fire back during the Civil War," said Sal. "Plus, we figured out the neighbor guy couldn't have done most of the stuff, so we knew it had to be a ghost…or whatever it is you are."

"And we talked to Katie," said Sofi.

"And that's it," I said. "We didn't mean to cause you any trouble, we just wanted to have fun here at the farm. Now it's your turn—why is the watch a secret?"

Chapter 27
The Confession

Noah sighed. "I have a confession to make. No one else in the whole world knows about it, except for Katie."

"Why don't you just start at the beginning," said Sal.

Noah sighed again. "My name is Noah Wheeler, and this is my sister Katie," he said. "My father was an Abolitionist, working to bring an end to slavery. We traveled from Boston, where I was born, to Kansas Territory. Papa took a position at a new university near our farm."

"In Lawrence? Kansas University?" I asked.

Noah shook his head. "There was no university in Lawrence. Baker University was south of the farm a few miles. Papa taught Greek and Latin there."

"It's still there!" I said. "That's where my Aunt Abby teaches!"

"Your aunt?" said Noah. He gave me a funny look. "A woman teaches there?"

I started to answer, but Ollie interrupted. "Just let him go on!"

"I wanted to return to Boston so I could attend Harvard, a university where my Uncle Wesley had a position. I spent hours reading Greek and Latin, and I studied mathematics every day, preparing to go to Harvard. I hoped to become a teacher like Papa and Uncle Wesley.

"But Papa wanted me to stay in Kansas and attend Baker. He said it was a fine institution and I would have many opportunities once I completed the curriculum. He said when the war was over, the new states and territories would need educated men to bring learning to the people who would settle the land."

Noah's voice got quieter as he went on.

"I argued with Papa every day, but he wouldn't agree. So I thought of a plan." Katie put her arms around Noah's shoulders. "I would get the money to pay my way to Boston, and Papa wouldn't be able to stop me."

"What did you do?" asked Sal.

"Something…very wrong." Noah's voice was almost a whisper. "I knew I should not have done it, but I was desperate to get away."

Katie was patting Noah on the back and comforting him. "Just tell them," she said. "You'll feel better."

"I took my father's silver pocket watch," said Noah. "It was worth a lot of money. I was going to sell it that day…the day of the fire."

"This old thing?" asked Ollie. He dangled the watch from its chain.

Noah nodded. He looked really miserable. "Papa treasured it."

"So why was it in the cellar?" I asked.

"Papa had said I could go with him to Lawrence that day," he said. "The night before, I took the watch off the chest by his bed and wrapped it in a rag. I hid it in a bowl behind a loose rock in the cellar. When we got to Lawrence, I was going to sneak away to the jeweler's and sell it. Then I could get on a riverboat for Kansas City and on to St. Louis. I would have been gone before Papa even missed me."

"So…what happened the day of the fire?" asked Sal.

Noah heaved a huge sigh. "I was in the barn, milking the cow, and Katie was gathering eggs. Papa was hitching the horse to the wagon in the barnyard. I was angry because he had told me yet again that morning that I had to stay in Kansas. But I had to go with him to Lawrence, so I could sell the watch. As soon as we finished breakfast, I was going to get it from the cellar.

"I heard horses arriving, and thought it was some

neighbors, but then I heard shouting, and a man asking Papa questions. I heard a gunshot and started to go look, but then I smelled smoke. I shoved Katie toward the door and slapped the cow to make her run. Then some burning hay fell beside me."

Nobody said a word. It was one of the worst things we'd ever heard.

"I tried to smother it with a horse blanket but I burned my hands and my shirt caught fire. The smoke was so thick I couldn't breathe. I got down and crawled, and I saw that the door was open, so I thought Katie had made it outside…."

He stopped for a second and pressed his fingers into his eyes. I'm pretty sure I saw a tear slide down his cheek. He wiped it away. "I made it to the door somehow, but when I looked out, all I saw was the wagon standing there. The men and horses, and Papa, were all gone. Then I saw Katie on the ground outside the barn door with broken eggshells all around her. And that's all I remember until…afterward."

"What do you mean, 'afterward?'" I asked.

"Somehow, I could see what was happening, as if I were dreaming," said Noah, "except I knew Katie and I would not wake up."

"No!" cried Ollie. "You said Katie got out, and you made it to the door!"

Sofi looked ready to cry.

"It was too late for us," said Noah. "The smoke and heat burned our lungs so badly we couldn't survive. My mother came running from the cabin, holding my baby brother. She found Katie and me in the barnyard. She cried and cried. Later that day a neighbor came to help her bury us near the river."

"So you don't know about your dad?" asked Sal.

"Only that he never came back to the farm," said Noah.

"He got killed by Quantrill!" said Ollie before I could stop him.

Noah got very still but said nothing for a minute. Then he asked, "How do you know?"

"From an old lady who's lived around here forever," I said. "She knew the Wheeler family lived here and the kids got caught in the barn fire. She said their dad was killed by Quantrill's raiders, and their mom took the baby and moved away to Topeka."

Katie buried her head in Noah's shoulder. He patted her on the back and said, "I hope my brother had a long and happy life."

"And now our uncle says the barn is haunted!" added Ollie.

Noah looked alarmed at that. "Surely he doesn't know about us?" he asked.

"He doesn't believe it," I said. "It's just a story that's been going around all these years. But he told us about how Quantrill's gang burned Lawrence and killed a bunch of men and boys, then went around hunting other free-staters."

"So that is why they came to our farm," said Noah. "Because Papa was an Abolitionist."

"My uncle said they probably didn't know you were in the barn," I added.

"So why were you mad at me?" asked Ollie. "You should've been mad at Quantrill and all those bad men!"

Noah was quiet for so long I thought he wasn't going to answer. But then he spoke up.

"I was. Those men did an evil thing, not just to Papa, and me and Katie, but to my mother and brother. But finally my anger died away and instead I thought only of how I could have changed that terrible day."

Chapter 28
Noah's Regrets

"**W**hat could you change?" asked Ollie.

"I could have put the watch back on Papa's dresser. I could have agreed to stay in Kansas, like he wanted. I could have looked out when the men came that morning—but I was angry, and closed the barn door. Katie might have lived if I had left it open."

"But then they would've taken you, too!" said Sal. "Orion's uncle said they were gonna kill every boy tall enough to hold a rifle! That wouldn't have made anything better!"

"But I would change what I said to him!" cried Noah. "Instead of my angry words, I would tell him how much I loved him, and how sorry I was for stealing the watch..."

"Maybe he never knew you took it," I said.

"Oh, he knew it was missing," said Noah, "but he would never suspect me. He trusted me…and I didn't deserve it."

"But what's so bad about me finding it?" asked Ollie.

"Don't you see?" asked Noah. His eyes flashed, and for a minute I thought the mad, mean Noah from the night before was back. But then he calmed down. "The watch reminded me that I'd been a bad son. Papa would have forgiven me, but…I was ashamed. I wanted it to stay hidden forever. When you found it, I lashed out at you. For that I am sorry. After you put out the fire in the barn, I realized how close I had come to doing something far worse than stealing the watch."

He looked at Ollie. "You may not believe me, but I truly just wanted to scare you. I thought if I smashed the toy blocks and pulled on the rope in the barn, I could force you to leave. When that failed, I opened the door of the chickens' roost, thinking your uncle would blame you and send you away. But no matter what I did, you were still here.

"Then that night…I gathered all my strength and made the barn shake, but you said you weren't afraid, so I did the worst thing I could think of. I started a fire. Can you forgive me?"

Sal, Ollie and I all looked at each other. Finally, Ollie

said, "I guess so," and turned the watch over in his hand. "So that's his name on the back?"

"A. J. Wheeler," said Noah. "He was a kind man with the highest of principles. He was proud to teach at Baker because the president of the university was also an Abolitionist who believed in freedom for all. Papa carried on the work of Mr. John Brown, who helped so many escape from slavery."

"John Brown!" said Ollie. "The guy who fought at Black Jack?"

"Yes," said Noah. "Papa greatly admired him."

"Did you ever meet him?" I asked. "John Brown?"

"Only once," said Noah. "Soon after we arrived here. He came to speak with Papa to make sure he could be trusted with his important work. After that, whenever runaways came for help, we hid them in the cellar."

In the cellar?!

"Did you see any runaways?" asked Ollie.

"Of course," said Noah. "I brought them food and water, and warm blankets in the winter. They told me amazing stories of how they escaped, and the hardships they endured, all in the hope of a better life."

"Awesome!" cried Sal. "You were part of the Underground Railroad!"

"You and your dad were heroes," I said. "The Underground Railroad's in our history books!"

"*I* was not heroic," said Noah. "The true heroes were

the brave people who escaped from slavery, even though they were frightened and in danger of being captured."

"You know there's no more slavery, right?" asked Sal.

"I hoped so," said Noah. "I saw after a time that no more fugitives came looking for help. It doesn't change what happened to Papa, but it helps to know he died for a worthy cause."

"And so did you!" I said.

For the first time, Katie spoke up.

"I'm glad you came to the farm," she said. "It's lonely, staying up by the river and in the trees."

"I'm glad, too," said Sofi.

"I know it is lonely for Katie," said Noah. "We stay away from the farmhouse and the people who live there. Even so, I can see that life has changed in many ways from when we lived."

"Yeah, it has," said Sal. "Remember we told you we've met ghosts before? We found a Native American boy from the 1840s in my house, and he was freaked out by all the stuff he saw!"

Noah looked confused. "Native American?" he asked.

"Uh, Indian!" said Sal. "He was a Wyandot!"

Noah nodded, then said, "Tell me, is it proper for girls to dress like you?"

Sofi and I laughed. "Everybody wears shorts in the summer!" I said.

Noah looked at Sal, who just shrugged. "And you truly go to school?" he asked. "When we came to Kansas Territory, it was unusual for girls to get schooling beyond the primary years, but Baker admitted women at the university level. Papa hoped that Katie would one day go there."

"Of course, girls go to school!" I said. "Women do everything men do! They're doctors and teachers and… and even on the Supreme Court!"

Noah looked so shocked I had to laugh! "Is that true?" he asked Sal.

"Uh, yeah," said Sal. "Remember, her aunt teaches at Baker."

"If only I had listened to Papa," said Noah. "He believed I could do great things if I stayed in Kansas and worked to spread freedom. I wanted more than anything to make him proud of me. But I never got the chance."

He sounded so sad I could hardly stand it. I suddenly thought about the stories Uncle Jeff had told us about my dad when he was a kid. "It was wrong to steal the watch," I said, "but it didn't make you a bad son. Your dad was a kid once, just like you. I bet he'd understand about the watch."

"Do you think so?" he asked. He looked so hopeful, I knew he *so* wanted to believe it.

"Absolutely," said Sal. "And he had to be proud of you for helping all those people on their way to freedom."

I thought of something else. *What was the name of the family that helped Susie Chase and her mom?* I squeezed my eyes shut and tried to remember Susie's story of how she got away…what was the farmer's name? *Hayes!*

"Noah," I said, "was there a family around here named Hayes?"

He looked surprised, but then said, "Mr. Hayes and his family lived several miles east of here, where the Wakarusa meets the Kaw."

"The Kaw?" asked Sal.

"The Kansas River!" I said. "That's another name for it! You know what this means, don't you? Maybe Susie and her mom came right by here! How wild is that?"

"Awesome!" cried Ollie.

Noah gave me a blank look, so I explained. "Susie Chase and her mom escaped from slavery in Missouri, and we found her in my great-grandma's attic. She told us Mr. and Mrs. Hayes helped them, and—"

"And she's our great-great-great-something aunt!" said Ollie.

"Oh," said Noah, nodding, "that explains it. You are the descendants of slaves."

"Yeah, we are!" I said proudly.

It was so exciting to hear about real life in the days

of the Underground Railroad! I was dying to hear more, but we heard a whistle from outside the trees. Barker lifted his head and wagged his tail.

"That's Uncle Jeff, whistling for Barker!" I said. "We have to go now!"

"We're going home tomorrow," said Ollie. "Can we talk to you one more time? Maybe when we feed the chickens tonight?"

I could tell Noah wasn't sure this was a good idea, but Katie smiled and looked so happy, he finally agreed. The rest of us turned and crawled back out through the underbrush. I blinked in the sunshine and looked back where we'd come from. All I saw were trees, vines and bushes. You'd never know Noah and Katie were there.

"Look!" cried Sofi as she pointed at the bare branches of the dead tree sticking up above the green leaves. There, near the very top, a hawk was sitting perfectly still. Call me crazy, but I was sure it was Samuel Grayhawk, keeping watch over us.

Chapter 29
Making It Up to Jeremiah ~ *and* ~ One Last Visit

Our hands, knees and clothes were muddy, we had leaves in our hair, and scratches on our arms and legs.

"We can't let Aunt Abby see us like this," I said, "'cause we weren't supposed to be in the trees."

"The rain barrel!" said Ollie. "We can wash up there."

We cleaned up the best we could, then sat under the walnut trees to talk about what we'd heard.

"So, Ollie," said Sal, "how does it feel to know *you're* the ghost magnet?"

"I'm not a ghost magnet!" he said. "And I still don't really understand why Noah stealing the watch made him do mean things to me!"

"He was mad at himself," said Sal. "The watch reminded him he'd done something bad, so he didn't want to ever see it again. Then when you found it, he took it out on you."

"Uh, OK," said Ollie.

"The things he did at first didn't work, so he ramped it up—pushing you in the river, messing with the hay pyramid," I said.

"I wish he would've just told me," said Ollie.

Just then Uncle Jeff came out the back door with Jeremiah, so we followed them to the barn.

"Take Barker and go look at the river while I unload the truck," Uncle Jeff said to Jeremiah. "Let me know if the water's started to go down."

Jeremiah nodded and walked off up the path. That gave me an idea.

"Can we go with him? To see the river?" I asked.

"Stay back from the water," said Uncle Jeff, "and don't get in the way."

Jeremiah and Barker were almost to the blueberry patch, so we ran to catch up. We stayed behind them as they started down the zig-zag path.

We already knew the water was high because we'd heard it rushing through the trees earlier. Now we followed Jeremiah far enough to see the river washing up over its banks. The waterfall was gone, and the dead tree bridge and the rock shelf we'd sat on had disappeared under the gray, murky water. Tree limbs and big logs floated on the current. I couldn't believe it was the same place we'd splashed and played only the day before.

Jeremiah took some photos of the river on his phone, then turned back and met us on the path. We stepped to the side to let him through. This was my chance.

"Uh, Jeremiah?" I said as he passed me. When he stopped and turned to face me, he seemed like just a regular teenage boy, not sneaky or mean or anything. Suddenly I wasn't sure what to say, but Ollie came to the rescue.

"Are you a body-builder?" he asked.

"You've got killer muscles, dude!" added Sal.

After a second Jeremiah broke into a smile. "I work out some." Then he took something out of his pocket and handed it to Ollie. When Ollie opened his hand, he held a red Lego astronaut.

"You found it!" cried Ollie. He did a happy dance, but Jeremiah just turned back around and started walking up the path. I tried again.

"Uh, Jeremiah?" I said. "Thanks…for everything."

He slowed in the middle of a step but didn't turn around. I'm pretty sure I heard him say, "You're welcome" as he headed for the barn. Uncle Jeff was waiting by the pickup truck to take him home.

Aunt Abby cooked a special dinner that night because we were going home in the morning: meat loaf, mashed potatoes and green beans from the garden. Ollie made a face when Uncle Jeff passed him the green beans.

"You'll like them this way," said Uncle Jeff. "There's bacon in them. Try them and see." He put about five green beans on Ollie's plate.

Ollie tried one of the beans, then ate them all! "Can I have some more?" he asked. Uncle Jeff laughed and spooned some more beans onto his plate.

Aunt Abby said she hoped we'd had fun at the farm, and asked us what our favorite things had been. Naturally, we couldn't talk about Noah and Katie, but we all came up with something.

"The tornado!" said Sal. "I thought it would be boring here, but that was pretty exciting!"

Sofi said she liked petting the chickens and Barker. Ollie said he liked flying the drone and playing in the hayloft. I said I liked running around the farm paths and swimming at the river. I really just wanted to get dinner over with so we could go feed and water the chickens one last time.

KATIE WASN'T SITTING UNDER THE NESTS WHEN WE SWEPT OUT THE ROOST. I was worried Noah had changed his mind about coming to see us, but as we closed the door on the chickens, we saw a glow in one of the back stalls.

"They're here!" Ollie whooped and ran to see. Noah and Katie were sitting on a bale of straw, hidden from the open barn door. We sat down too, and Katie moved over to sit between Sofi and Ollie.

"This is goodbye," I said, "'cause we're going home tomorrow."

"Will you be here when we come to get our pumpkins?" asked Sal. "Where are you when we can't see you?"

Noah hesitated. "I'll do my best to explain," he said. "Because of Ollie, you see us, but we are not really here. To most others, we don't exist. Your aunt and uncle don't see Katie watching over the chickens. They don't see me gazing at the river, thinking of where it might have taken me."

"But you said I summoned you!" said Ollie. "How do I do that?"

Noah shrugged. "All I know is that when you arrived, I could tell one of you had the ability to see us. I couldn't hide from you, so I tried to make you leave. But I've promised Katie—and myself—that if someone like you comes again, I will not try to frighten them away."

"So, will you just be here...or not...forever?" asked Sal.

Noah looked out toward the barn door. "I wanted nothing more than to get away from this farm, but now

I can never leave it." Somehow that seemed the saddest thing of all.

"What do you want me to do with the watch?" asked Ollie.

"Please put it back in the cellar," said Noah. "That way it will always belong to Papa."

I don't think that's what Ollie wanted to hear, but he said, "OK."

"Will we ever see you again?" asked Sofi.

"Can we?" asked Katie, looking up at Noah.

"I think not," said Noah. "I know now you came in friendship and I'm grateful that you treated me and Katie with kindness, but it is best that we part ways. And…I am glad you didn't let me frighten you away." I saw a sad smile on Noah's face.

"But what about next time we come to see our aunt and uncle?" I asked. I couldn't stand the thought of never seeing them again! It would be so great, getting to know them the way we did with Samuel and Susie.

"No," said Noah. "Our story is written and as you said, cannot be changed. Yours lies ahead of you. We'll live on in your memories, and that is enough."

"I'm so sorry about what happened to you, and I'll never forget you!" I said, and the others all agreed. But before we could say anything else, Noah and Katie's glow began to get dimmer. They faded away right before our eyes.

Chapter 30
The Penny

It was a busy evening. We had to get ready to go home the next day. Sofi and I sorted and folded the clean laundry while Ollie and Sal vacuumed the bedrooms. We tidied up the bathroom and put our cousins' things back where they belonged (except for the Ouija board). Then we went to watch a movie with Aunt Abby and Uncle Jeff.

"It sure was fun having kids around this week," said Aunt Abby. "We'll see you again when you come to get your pumpkins at Halloween."

"You know," I said, "I can't believe what an interesting place the farm is—I never knew so many cool things happened right here!"

"Ollie, I thought the battlefield would be your favorite thing," said Uncle Jeff. "Didn't you like it?"

"Oh…yeah," said Ollie, "but I was thinking about the battles you told us about, and all the bad things that happened to people, like, you know, the kids who were in the barn when it got burned. Do you think that happens a lot?"

"Absolutely," said Uncle Jeff. "It's not just soldiers who get wounded or killed. Innocent people, including children, lose their homes, their parents, even their lives sometimes."

I'm not sure Ollie had ever thought about wars that way before. He didn't say anything more about it.

"Remember what you told us about John Brown helping runaway slaves?" I asked. "Wouldn't it be cool if he brought some of them here?"

"I've wondered if he did," said Aunt Abby. "The cellar would be a good hiding place, but we'll probably never know."

Oh, but we do!

After we watched our movie, Sofi and Ollie sat in Bailey's room with the Ouija board between them. "Will we ever see Noah and Katie again?" asked Ollie.

Nothing happened. The pointer didn't move at all, and at first I thought maybe Sofi was pushing down on it too hard. But then it started creeping up the board. It hovered in the middle and then finally went to the word "NO." I hadn't realized I'd been holding my breath.

Ollie's shoulders slumped. "Dang," he said. "I really wanted to see them again!"

"Well," said Sal, "you're the one who can do it, right? You've got the power to…uh…commune with spirits."

"But I don't know *how* I do it!" said Ollie. "And anyway, I only think it works if the spirit *wants* to be communed with, or whatever."

Ollie pushed the pointer back to the middle of the board. "Will Mom and Dad let me get my own drone?" he asked. I couldn't believe it, but the pointer moved to "YES."

Sal was so excited by that, he tried it too. "How about me?" he asked. "Will I get a drone?" Again, the pointer moved to "YES."

"I hate to tell you guys, but it's probably lying," I said. "Don't get your hopes up."

By this time it was totally dark, so we went through Brent's room and out to the porch. After the clouds and rain the night before, the sky was so clear you could see millions—maybe billions—of stars.

"Look," said Sofi. "There's no light in the barn."

I heard Uncle Jeff's voice from the hallway. "Is everyone ready for tomorrow?" he asked as he came out and stood on the porch with us.

"We were just looking at all the stars we can see out

here!" I said. "Look, there's the Big Dipper." I showed Sofi where to look. "See? It's upside down."

"See the white streaks in the sky?" said Uncle Jeff. "That's the Milky Way. I bet you've never seen that from where you live!"

All of a sudden I felt really wiped out. We trooped back into the house and got ready for bed.

MY FIRST THOUGHT WHEN I WOKE UP SATURDAY MORNING WAS, *I'm going home today*! This time yesterday I'd been so keyed up about Katie and Noah, I didn't even think about going home, but now I was happy and excited. Yeah, I'd had fun at the farm, but I was ready to sleep in my own bed, talk to my friends, and get ready for sixth grade. I slid out of bed and called to Sofi. She opened her eyes and sat up smiling.

"Get dressed so we can go home!" I said.

When we got to the kitchen, Ollie and Sal were already there, eating cinnamon rolls.

"Look what Aunt Abby made!" said Ollie. "You better hurry or we're gonna eat them all!"

Sofi and I each grabbed a roll. Ollie and Sal were already on their second one. Uncle Jeff came in the kitchen and said, "Everybody ready for the trip home?" We all just nodded 'cause our mouths were full.

"Don't forget to bring your blueberries up from the cellar," said Aunt Abby.

"We won't!" said Ollie. I knew he was really think-ing about putting the watch back behind the rock.

So, we finished our cinnamon rolls and went to the cellar. Everybody grabbed a bucket of blueberries and took it upstairs, then we went back down the steps. I was about to explode.

"Just think of it!" I said. "Noah said runaway slaves stayed here in this cellar—*right where we're standing!*"

"Awesome!" said Sal. We all just looked around the cellar, imagining what it was like back then. But we didn't have much time.

"I guess I have to put the watch back," said Ollie. He pulled it out of his pocket and we handed it around one last time. Then he pulled the old bowl out from behind the loose rock and wrapped the watch in the rag.

"Is it tingling?" I asked.

"No," he said. He laid it carefully in the bowl, but suddenly looked up. "There's something in the bottom of the bowl."

He moved the rag aside. The bottom of the bowl was crusted with dirt, but he dug his fingers in and then held up what looked like a dirty brown coin.

Sal took it, spit on his finger and rubbed one side of it clean. We saw the words "one cent" in the dim light.

"Just a penny," said Sal. He sounded disappointed. Ollie put the penny in his pocket and pushed the bowl as far into the wall as he could. No one would ever guess it was there. We took the last of the blueberries and went back upstairs.

Chapter 31
Farewell to the Farm

After one last trip to the hayloft, we hugged Barker goodbye. Sofi went to pet the chickens while we loaded our stuff in the SUV.

"It's going to seem quiet here without you kids," said Aunt Abby as we turned onto the highway. "I hope you'll come back to stay again!"

BACK HOME, MR. AND MRS. MARTELLI WERE WAITING at our house with Mom and Dad. Mr. Martelli thanked Uncle Jeff and Aunt Abby for letting Sal and Sofi visit the farm. "I'm sure it was a real eye-opening experience for them," he said.

If you only knew...

Sal went on and on about the tornado, and Sofi ran

across the street to see Coco, her calico cat. Ollie went in to get Butterscotch and the grownups went inside to talk, so Sal and I sat on the front porch.

"So what do you think?" he asked. "I mean, about... you know."

"Well," I said, "this might sound crazy, but it's almost like I was on a different planet last week."

"I know what you mean," he said. "It's like, now that it's over, it feels like it happened to somebody else, and I was just watching."

"Well, now it's back to real life," I said. "I mean, school starts in four days."

"That's right," he said. "I think I'll call Alex to see if he wants to hang out. Take it easy." He got up and walked across the street while I went in the house to tell Aunt Abby and Uncle Jeff goodbye.

AFTER MY AUNT AND UNCLE LEFT, I went up to my room to unpack. I caught my breath as I walked in my door. I'd completely forgotten Mom and Dad were painting my room! The fresh lavender walls looked wonderful, and my new bedspread was awesome! I ran downstairs to tell Mom how much I loved it.

Later that night I was sitting on my bed, loving the way my room looked and thinking what else I could do to make it special for sixth grade. Maybe I could frame some of my drawings. Ollie came over and sat on my bed.

"Get your feet off the bedspread," I said.

He was holding the dirty penny he'd found in the bowl in Uncle Jeff's cellar. "This penny's weird," he said.

"It looks OK to me," I said. But up close, I saw there really *was* something different about it. I licked my finger and rubbed it hard. We both gasped. Instead of Abraham Lincoln on the front, there was…an Indian chief? And the date at the bottom said *1860*!

"Oh, my God!" I said. "This is really *old!*" We took the penny into the bathroom and washed it under the faucet. It was pretty worn, but we could read all the words and see the spiky feathers on the Indian's head.

"Do we have to give it back to Uncle Jeff?" asked Ollie.

"Well…it really does belong to them," I said. "I guess we should tell Mom and Dad."

Ollie looked disappointed, but said, "I guess so."

We went downstairs to show the penny to Mom and Dad. Ollie told them he'd found it in the cellar at Uncle Jeff's (leaving out a few important details, lol). Dad was really excited about it.

"This is a very rare coin," he said. "There aren't many of them left in existence."

"Will Uncle Jeff let me keep it?" asked Ollie.

"We'll tell him about it and see what he thinks," said Dad.

THE NEXT NIGHT AT DINNER, Dad told us he'd talked to Uncle Jeff about the penny.

"He said it was probably buried down there for over a hundred years, and Aunt Abby said Ollie deserves to keep it."

Ollie whooped and pumped his fist. "Awesome!" he cried. "I can't wait to go back to the farm! My pumpkin's gonna be SO big by Halloween!"

"How about you?" Mom asked me. "I know you didn't want to go to the farm, but it sounds like you had a good time. What did you learn while you were there?"

What to say? "Uh…well, a lot, actually," I said. "How to take care of chickens, how to fly a drone, a lot about the Underground Railroad… "

"And what a tornado's really like!" said Ollie.

"Speaking of tornadoes," said Dad, "where exactly were you that night? Uncle Jeff said there's something you need to tell us."

Busted! I squirmed a little. "Well…the night of the tornado, we snuck out to the barn 'cause Ollie left his Legos out there, then the storm started and the power went out, then it rained and hailed a lot and we couldn't go back to the house." I gave Ollie the evil eye.

"Yeah, it was because of me," he said.

"Do you understand why that wasn't a good decision?" asked Mom.

"Yeah, but it wasn't raining when we left the house,

and we thought we'd be right back! We didn't mean to make them worry!" said Ollie.

"But Uncle Jeff did tell us to stay in the house," I said. "We messed up."

"Well, you didn't know there was going to be a tornado," said Dad, "but I hope you learned to stop and think about the consequences before you do something. What if the tornado had hit the barn?"

"Or what if you got struck by lightning?" asked Mom. "Storms can be dangerous."

"Don't worry, I didn't know that then, but I know it now!" I said.

Chapter 32
I'm Still Me

The next few days flew by. School was starting later in the week, and there was so much to do, I never talked to Sal again about our "adventure" with Noah and Katie. He was right, it *was* like it happened to a different person. We just kind of moved on from it.

The night before school started I sat on my bed, thinking how different things were from a year ago, when I started fifth grade. I mean, *I'm* different. Last year I didn't even believe in ghosts, but now I've met three different kinds—a "regular" ghost, a spirit, and two phantoms.

It's funny, you wouldn't think dead people have much to do with your everyday life, but they do! I'd learned a lot from Samuel and Susie about being a good sister and a good friend. But Noah Wheeler had made me think about things I'd *never* thought of before.

First of all, what if my mom or dad died? I mean, I'd be sad, but it's more complicated than that. Like, when my dad left for work this morning, I just said, "Bye, Dad," and didn't even look up. What if those were the last words I ever spoke to him? It helped me see why Noah was so angry, knowing he'd never be able to tell his dad he was sorry for stealing the watch. I'd never want to feel guilty about something forever!

I also decided it's good to talk about your feelings with someone (well...*almost* always—you don't have to tell everybody else who you *like*, lol). Noah kept all that sadness and anger bottled up inside him for over a hundred years, and it made him into a sad, angry person...I mean, phantom. I hope talking about it with us made him feel better about himself.

Seeing what happened with Noah also showed me that when you do something to hurt someone else, it hurts *you*, because you're not being the best person you can be. I mean, look what I did just in the last week—I trash-talked my brother and blamed Jeremiah for bad things just because he seemed different. I can be better than that! I want Mom and Dad to be proud of me, and I want to be proud of myself.

Then there was what Noah said about girls in school! What if somebody told me I couldn't go to school just because I'm a girl? That would suck! It reminded me of when Susie told us that slaves weren't allowed to learn to read. Nobody should ever keep people from learning things!

And you may not believe it, but I realized how much I like my little brother! The way he stood up to Noah showed me that you've gotta face your fears head-on (and it helps to have your friends watching your back). It's funny how things have changed between Ollie and me since last year. Yeah, I say he's a pain in the butt, but he's a pretty awesome kid! He's braver, and tougher, and smarter than I ever knew. I want to be the kind of sister for him that Samuel, Susie, and Noah would want me to be.

And if all this wasn't enough to think about, there was…drum roll…finding out I'm not the ghost magnet. I won't lie, that was *hard*. For almost a whole year I'd thought I had this superpower, but…I don't. And even worse, my brother has it! I was pretty jealous, and I cried about it a little bit alone in my room at night. But then I thought about what happened with Noah when he kept all those bad feelings bottled up inside. I knew I had to talk it out with somebody.

The question was, who? It couldn't be Mom or Dad or my friends, lol. I couldn't even talk about it with Sal, 'cause I'd never really admitted to him I thought I had the superpower. That left one person…Ollie. I jumped off my bed and went across the hall to his room. He was in bed with his lamp on, so I went in and closed the door behind me. Then I took a deep breath and poured it all out.

It's funny, I thought he'd act all big-headed about it, but he didn't. When I told him how mad I'd been that he was the ghost magnet and not me, he surprised me.

"Why is everybody always mad at *me* about it?" he said. "First Noah and now you? It's not like I *wanted* to be a ghost magnet!"

"But it's like a superpower!" I said. "*I* wanted it! It's something almost nobody else in the world has!"

"Yeah, it's cool," he said, "but I can't tell anybody about it, so really, what difference does it make? I'm still just me."

I had to laugh. "You know, you're right," I said as I ruffled his hair. "And I'm still me! I'll always be your big sister."

"You're not gonna let me forget it, are you?" he said.

I laughed again. "So, do you ever want to see another ghost?" I asked.

He thought a minute. "Maybe someday."

"You better go to sleep so you'll be ready for fourth grade tomorrow," I said as I got up to leave.

"How about you?" he asked as he switched off his lamp. "Do you want to see another one?"

"You know," I said before I closed his door, "ghosts,

spirits, phantoms…they're a lot harder to understand than I thought. If I never meet another one, that's fine by me."

Epilogue

Sixth grade started off with a bang! My days were filled with school, soccer practice, and hanging with my friends. I practiced running almost every day. I was back in the accelerated math class, because, in case you didn't know it, girls are just as good at math as boys!

On top of that, Mrs. Davidson from two streets over asked if I could watch her first-grader after school once in awhile. Mom gave me the talk about being responsible and mature, yada yada, but what I really took seriously were the things I'd learned from Samuel, Susie and Noah. Not just what they said, but what they did—the examples they set. I decided I want to set a good example, too, even if just for Ollie. Isn't it weird how much we can learn from ghosts? But remember, they were once just kids, like you and me.

Before I knew it, it was October again, time for the Shawnee Indian Mission's Fall Festival. Like last year, my mom and dad walked to the Mission grounds with Mr. and Mrs. Martelli. Ollie and I followed along, but as soon as we got there, I hunted down Mady and Taylor and we found a good spot to hang out. Ollie ran off with some boys from his class, and Sofi went with her mom to watch the Native dancing.

Sal was sitting on the ground with some boys from his baseball team. They were eating, talking and laughing.

"Do you think they're talking about sports or girls?" asked Mady as we walked by.

I giggled at the thought. I saw Sal whispering something to Alex, then they high-fived, paying no attention to us. But just for an instant—I swear—he caught my eye, raised one eyebrow, and kind of smiled. Then before I knew it, he was grinning at Alex and the moment was over.

But in that moment, I *knew* he was remembering how it all started, just a year ago, the night of the Fall Festival. And you know what? Even after Sal and Ollie and Sofi and I grow up and go our separate ways, we'll always remember our ghost adventures. Nobody can take those away from us.

Afterword

Places and Terms

The Wakarusa River is a tributary of the Kansas River, or Kaw. The rivers join in Douglas County, Kansas and flow eastward to join the Missouri. The Wakarusa was dammed in 1977 to reduce spring flooding.

The Battle of Black Jack took place June 2, 1856. John Brown and his men ambushed a group of pro-slavery men camped near a creek south of Lawrence, Kansas, a free-state stronghold. Just two weeks earlier, pro-slavery forces had sacked the city of Lawrence. They destroyed businesses, including two newspapers' printing presses. See https://civilwaronthewesternborder.org/encyclopedia/battle-black-jack

According to researchers, the Ouija board functions as a result of users' unconscious knowledge and ideas, called the ideomotor effect. This means that a person's unconscious mind can cause the muscles in their hands and arms to move in a certain way, even though they believe it is not voluntary. For more information, see https://www.rd.com/article/how-a-ouija-board-really-works/

The Abolition movement grew primarily in the large cities of the northeast United States in the early 1800s. It spread to the west after 1854 when it became apparent that Kansas Territory would be a major battleground in the fight to keep slavery from spreading to new states. An organization called the New England Emigrant Aid Company raised money to help people move to Kansas and work to make sure Kansas became a free state. The first group arrived from Massachusetts in 1854 and settled the town of Lawrence. See also: https://www.kshs.org/kansapedia/emigrant-aid-societies/16697

John Brown was a noted Abolitionist, active in the days of Bleeding Kansas. He guided runaway slaves from the border regions and took part in several military skirmishes leading up to the Civil War. A wall-size mural painted by artist John Steuart Curry for the Kansas Capitol Building shows John Brown holding a Bible and a rifle. Union and Confederate soldiers lie before him and a tornado rages in the background.

The Grover barn was built in 1858 by farmer Joel Grover in Douglas County, Kansas. Grover and his wife Emily were both part of the wave of Abolitionists who immigrated to Kansas from the east. The barn's use as a station on the Underground Railroad is well-documented. See also: https://ffnha.oncell.com/en/grover-barn-261579.html

More on the Grover Barn can be viewed on YouTube: Encounter on the Underground Railroad: Freedom Seekers & the Grover Barn (video produced by the Watkins Museum of History featuring historian Judy Sweets) at https://youtu.be/Gk4cmeEGI-o. Judy Sweets is the author of additional books and articles about the Kansas Territorial period and the Underground Railroad, including "Rev. John E. Stewart: Kansas Underground Railroad Agent Transformed by the Irrepressible Conflict," *Embattled Lawrence: The Enduring Struggle for Freedom, Vol 2*, Lawrence, Kansas, Dennis Domer, Editor, Watkins Museum of History, Lawrence, KS, 2023; and "The Underground Railroad in Douglas County, Kansas Territory," *John Brown Photo Chronology* (catalog of the exhibition at Harper's Ferry 2009), Jean Libby. Allies for Freedom publishers, Palo Alto, CA, 2009.

The autism spectrum is a measure of a developmental disability. According to the Centers for Disease Control and Prevention (CDC), it is caused by differences in the brain. "People with ASD may behave, communicate, interact, and learn in ways that are different from most other people. There is often nothing about how they look that sets them apart from other people." https://www.cdc.gov/ncbddd/autism/signs.html

"Quantrill's Raid" refers to the early-morning attack of Lawrence on August 21, 1863 by William Quantrill and a force of more than 400 men. They rode through the night to reach the city before dawn so they could surprise the inhabitants. They killed approximately 180 men and boys and looted the town. Some of the gang then rode through the surrounding areas attacking Abolitionist farms. See https://www.bakerhistoryblog.com/post/the-day-baldwin-city-and-baker-university-almost-burned

The note about Quantrill's order to kill every boy tall enough to hold a rifle is from a talk by historian Robert K. Sutton, keynote speaker for *Civil War on the Western Front* at Watkins Museum, Lawrence, Kansas, on August 19, 2017.

Estimates of the number of fugitives who came through Douglas County are from documents cited by Dr. Richard Sheridan, author of *Freedom's Crucible: The Underground Railroad in Lawrence and Douglas County, Kansas, 1854–1864, A Reader*. For photos and further information, see https://exhibits.lib.ku.edu/exhibits/show/quantrill/hell/horror.

Baker University was established as a four-year university in 1858 near Baldwin, three years before Kansas became a state. Unlike most universities of that time, Baker admitted women, and one of the first graduates was a woman. The first president, Werter Renick Davis, was an Abolitionist from Ohio who later led a volunteer cavalry unit during the Civil War. https://www.bakerhistoryblog.com/post/werter-renick-davis-the-first-president-1. Students at Baker in the 1860s were required to study Greek, Latin and mathematics.

Silver tarnishes, or becomes discolored, when exposed to air over time. Typically silver tarnishes to a dull black color.

Static electricity occurs when electrons that have built up on a surface discharge when they come into contact with another surface. A possible explanation for why the watch "shocked" Ollie is that after he petted Barker, he had excess electrons on his skin, which discharged when he touched the watch.

About the Author

Growing up in northeastern Kansas, Fran Borin soaked up the stories of the area's turbulent history, from the horrors of Indian removal and Bleeding Kansas to the hope of the Underground Railroad. After writing the first two Orion O'Brien Ghost Adventures, it seemed only natural to add the shocking tales of Quantrill's raid on Lawrence. *Orion O'Brien and the Phantoms of Wakarusa* shows how the diverse cultures that settled the territory—Native Americans, Blacks seeking freedom from slavery, and east-coast dwellers steeped in abolitionist fervor—worked together to make Kansas a free state. A graduate of Baker University, Fran knew the Wakarusa region would be the perfect stage on which to set the story.

Find more information on all the Ghost Adventures at orionkobrien.com.

www.ingramcontent.com/pod-product-compliance
Lightning Source LLC
Chambersburg PA
CBHW021139190726

48288CB00008B/2737